Ali swallowe

'I shall hand in r
job.'

'You would do that? Go to those lengths?'

'Yes, Connor, I would,' she said levelly.

'I see,' he said quietly. 'I had no idea you felt so strongly.'

He did move aside then to allow her to pass, but as she did so she felt a sharp pang as she caught sight of the pain in his eyes.

Laura MacDonald lives in the Isle of Wight. She is married and has a grown-up family. She has enjoyed writing fiction since she was a child, but for several years she worked for members of the medical profession, both in pharmacy and in general practice. Her daughter is a nurse and has helped with the research for Laura's medical stories.

Recent titles by the same author:

DRASTIC MEASURES

BY
LAURA MACDONALD

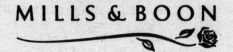

*First published in Great Britain 1996
Harlequin Mills & Boon Limited,
Eton House, 18-24 Paradise Road, Richmond, Surrey TW9 1SR*

© Laura MacDonald 1996

ISBN 0 263 80002 4

*Set in Times 10 on 11 pt. by
Rowland Phototypesetting Limited
Bury St Edmunds, Suffolk*

03-9701-48578-D

*Printed and bound in Great Britain
by Mackays of Chatham PLC, Chatham*

CHAPTER ONE

IT STARTED just like any other Monday morning, but if Ali had had any inkling of what was about to happen she wouldn't have left her house in Church Close to cycle to work. Instead, no doubt, she would have chosen to stay in bed. As it was, she arrived at the accident and emergency department at St Mark's Hospital just as she had on countless other mornings and, together with her colleagues, took over from the exhausted night shift.

'Sounds like they had a bad night,' she said to her fellow staff nurse, Maggie Hoskins, as the pair of them scrambled into their uniforms.

'Perhaps that will be followed by a quiet day,' replied Maggie hopefully, groaning as she caught sight of her reflection in the changing-room mirror.

'I shouldn't count on it.' Ali pulled a face.

'No,' Maggie sighed. 'From that hubbub in Reception it sounds as if the onslaught has already started. I'm sure people sit and plot what devilish situations they can devise to try the patience of us Casualty staff. Oh, by the way,' she added as she fastened her fob watch to the front of her uniform, 'did you know you have a student with you this morning?'

'That's all I need.' Ali straightened her cap and opened the door. 'Nothing I like better than a fresh-faced young student on a Monday morning, all scrubbed and eager. . .'

'Unless it's a stroppy, unwashed one who's had a bad weekend and doesn't want to be here,' observed Maggie drily.

'Oh, God, don't,' muttered Ali as they stepped out into the corridor and shut the door behind them. 'I couldn't bear it.'

'You might get that young Simon Bently—now, that would brighten up a dull Monday.' Maggie giggled.

'Don't be silly; he's still wet behind the ears,' said Ali.

'True,' agreed Maggie, 'but it could be fun teaching him.'

They were still giggling when they reached Reception, where they were met by Charge Nurse Harvey Gatten who informed Ali that Student Nurse Jessica Lake had been assigned to her.

'She's a good kid,' said Harvey, 'but a bit squeamish, apparently. Hasn't done A and E yet or Theatre.'

'Oh, great—thanks, Harvey,' said Ali.

'So not only will you have the patients throwing up this morning,' said Maggie cheerfully, 'it'll be the staff as well.'

'Push off, you!' Ali gave her friend a playful shove then, as Maggie grinned and hurried away, she stuck her head round the corner of the nurses' station so that she could see into Reception.

Already, in spite of the early hour, the rows of chairs were rapidly filling up and the receptionists beginning to look harassed. 'So where is Florence Nightingale?' asked Ali. 'I take it she has been told what time we start?'

'Oh, yes,' Harvey grinned. 'She was here at the crack of dawn—I got her checking supplies. She's in the store room—you'd better go and find her and tell her what you want her to do.'

To Ali's relief, Jessica Lake was one of the eager, fresh-faced variety of students and, just for one moment as she showed her round and began explaining how the system worked on the busy A and E unit, Ali found that the girl reminded her of herself—or rather how she had been eight years ago when she had been a newcomer to the nursing profession.

But that had been a long time ago and much water had flowed under the bridge since then. She was older, not so hot-headed, and, she hoped, not so easily taken in. Even as the thought crossed her mind she mentally pulled herself up. You're not only getting old, McKenzie, she told herself sharply, you're getting cynical as well.

'So, will we see all these patients this morning?' There was a note of disbelief in Jessica's voice.

'That's the general idea,' Ali nodded. 'If we can't, then I'm afraid some will just have to wait.'

'But how do we know? How do we know which ones can wait and which ones can't?'

'Ah, that's what we have to sort out,' replied Ali. 'That's what it's all about here in A and E. Assessment first, followed by identification and then intervention.'

'Sounds confusing,' said Jessica doubtfully.

'At first, maybe, but you'll soon get the hang of it.'

'How long have you been doing it?'

'What, nursing—' Jessica raised her eyebrows '—or Accident and Emergency?'

'Yes, Casualty.'

'I've been here at St Mark's for eighteen months and, before you ask, yes, I love it.'

'And where were you before that?'

'At a hospital in Suffolk—general surgical ward,' Ali replied, then broke off as there came the sound of a sudden commotion in Reception. 'Oh, looks like someone's collapsed,' she said. 'Come on, come and watch what happens.'

It was a youngish man who had collapsed following, according to the reception staff, a bout of aggressive behaviour. After the porters had carried him into a cubicle, it was quickly established from his property and his general condition that he was a diabetic. He had received his required dose of insulin but had not had any breakfast and had consequently gone into a hypoglycaemic state.

The casualty officer that morning was Samara Rahjid, who ordered an intravenous dextrose solution to be set up.

'This will restore his blood sugar levels,' explained Ali to Jessica as she set up the drip.

The morning wore on, the unit growing busier with the usual assortment of incidents—home-based accidents, road traffic accidents, accidents in the workplace and some patients with long-term complaints who were simply seeking a second opinion.

'Do you get many of those?' asked Jessica in apparent amazement as a man finished giving a history of a recurrent sore throat and was examined by the casualty officer before being advised to report back to his GP.

'You'd be surprised,' said Ali.

'But that's terrible,' said Jessica. 'They shouldn't waste valuable time like that.'

'Maybe not,' Ali replied, 'but sometimes it's a genuine cry for help when someone is absolutely at the end of their tether, so every case has to be assessed and evaluated.'

'Yes, but a sore throat!'

'We had someone once who presented with a sore throat and it turned out that it was a symptom of an impending heart attack,' said Ali, 'so, you see, it just goes to show you can't take anything on face value alone.'

'Ali,' called Harvey at that moment, 'there's a patient in cubicle two; he's cut his hand with a meat cleaver. Can you do an assessment, please?'

'Oh, my God,' whispered Jessica, but she stoically followed Ali into the cubicle.

Later, looking back on that morning, Ali was able to pinpoint precisely at what moment it happened—just as people, years later, were able to say exactly what they had been doing when they first heard news of great importance. Only this time it wasn't news—it was a voice and, watched intently by Jessica, she had just finished removing sutures from a young girl's hand.

Afterwards, she could even recall in detail what the girl had been wearing, but at the time she was only conscious of the impact of hearing that voice again. And not only hearing it, but identifying it amidst all the others in Reception. It was a voice she knew well, which wasn't surprising really because she had carried the sound of it around in her head for the past three years. But hearing it now in Reception, it was as familiar as if it had only been the day before that she had last heard it.

She also knew that she had frozen, apparently rooted to the spot—possibly for a full minute—tweezers in one hand and kidney-shaped dish in the other.

'Ali?' Jessica looked up and frowned. 'Is there something wrong?'

She took a deep breath, struggling to regain her composure. 'I don't know,' she muttered at last. 'That's something I need to find out. Here, get rid of this.' She thrust the dish and tweezers into Jessica's hands and from somewhere summoned the courage to draw back the cubicle curtains.

He was standing at the reception desk and at her first sight of him her heart twisted painfully, just as it had done so many times in the past. He was talking to Chrissie, no doubt charming her in the way only he knew how. She was vaguely aware that Maggie was standing behind Chrissie, a set of records in her hand, but Ali's main concern was the man at the desk.

His back was half turned towards her, but to Ali he looked the same as he had always done. He was dressed in denim jeans and a tan jacket in soft leather, his white shirt casually open at the neck. The dark tangle of his hair, she noticed, he still wore a little longer than was fashionable so that it curled against his collar and around his ears.

Chrissie was laughing at something he had just said, gazing up at him, the look on her face one that Ali had seen so many times before on the faces of so many other women. She knew that if he turned she would see the same lean, pale face, the sensual curve of his lips and the piercing blue of his eyes. Those same eyes with their smudged fringe of smoky lashes that had so attracted, fascinated, mesmerised her, all to her cost.

But, she asked herself even as, motionless, she watched, what the hell was he doing? Here in Denehurst, of all places? Was he merely passing through? Was he a patient? Had an accident, perhaps? He didn't look as if he'd been involved in an accident. He looked casual and relaxed. Damn him.

Even as the questions teemed in her mind he turned, his reaction suggesting that he knew he was being watched, but then as he caught sight of her and the blue eyes met hers the surprise that flared there was unmistakable.

'Ali?' he said wonderingly.

Just for one, brief, crazy moment it was as if the clock had been turned back at least three years, probably five, as they stared at each other and relived the past.

'Connor.' Somehow, heaven only knew how, she managed to nod; to appear normal.

'Well, this is a surprise,' he said, then, glancing at Chrissie, he moved away from the desk towards Ali.

As he covered the distance between them with his long, easy stride Ali knew a moment of blind panic. She didn't want to speak to him. Didn't even want to see him. Damn it, hadn't she spent the last three years trying to forget him, trying to eradicate all traces of him? And here he was again, as large as life, with that same maddening look in his eyes—a look both faintly questioning but at the same time charged with amusement—as he strolled back into her life as casually as if there had never been anything between them.

'So, what brings you to this neck of the woods?' she asked. To her utter amazement her voice came out naturally, sounded quite normal in fact, in spite of the turmoil that was going on inside her. Out of the corner of her eye she saw that Maggie had stopped reading the records she was holding and was watching what was going on with interest.

'Sheer luck, I should imagine.' He was standing directly in front of her now and gazing down at her, his eyes travelling over her. 'Either that, or the most fortunate of coincidences.'

'I'm amazed you should think so,' she said crisply, at the same time hoping desperately that her voice sounded firm and wasn't quavering. He knew her so well and would pick up any trace of emotion.

'You've had your hair cut,' he said softly, apparently choosing to ignore the implication behind her remark.

'I've worn it like this for a long time,' she said quickly, her intention being to remind him just how much time had passed.

'I like it.' Again, he appeared to be choosing to ignore any innuendo.

'You always preferred long hair,' she retorted.

'People change.' His reply was loaded and she knew it, but before she could respond further he leaned closer to her and as she caught the scent of him a sense of familiarity washed over her and the breath caught in her throat. 'You look lovely, Ali,' he murmured.

From somewhere, she had no idea where, she found her voice. 'You still haven't said what. . .what you are doing here,' she faltered at last.

'Ah, no,' he said, his eyes still roaming—over her face, her hair and coming at last to rest on her mouth, 'I haven't, have I?'

She found that she was holding her breath as she waited for his explanation, an explanation which, however, wasn't to come for at that moment Harvey called to her from the nurses' station.

'Ali—road traffic accident arriving. Estimated time of arrival was five minutes, but that was four minutes ago. It's a bad one. You and Maggie—outside, please.'

She moved forward automatically, her years of training taking over as, carefully sidestepping Connor, she joined Maggie and together they pushed open the double doors.

As they stepped outside into the warm May sunshine an ambulance, its blue light flashing, turned in at the gates.

'Handsome guy,' murmured Maggie out of the side of her mouth, without taking her eyes off the approaching vehicle.

'If you like that sort of thing.' Ali's attempt at nonchalance was deliberate.

'Oh, I do, I do,' Maggie replied, visibly bracing herself as the ambulance screeched to a halt in front of them. 'I take it you know him.' There was an intensely curious note in her voice.

'I should do,' Ali replied and as the paramedics jumped from the ambulance, she moved forward swiftly to join them.

'What do you mean?' asked Maggie as one of the

paramedics opened the doors and secured them and the other disappeared inside.

'What I say,' replied Ali calmly. 'You asked if I know him—I said I should do.' Her mouth tightened. 'You get to know someone pretty well if you live with them for a couple of years.' She paused and then, glancing at the second paramedic, she said, 'What do we have, Mac?'

'Motorbike had a disagreement with an articulated lorry,' replied Tony MacPherson tersely. 'Head and chest injuries for the girl pillion. The boy has arrested twice.'

'Right, let's get him inside at the double.' Vaguely Ali was aware of Maggie's astonished look, then the sheer urgency of the situation took over as they escorted the badly injured couple into one of the emergency treatment rooms.

The casualty officer, Samara Rahjid, was already in the room, together with Harvey, Staff Nurse Beth Rawlings, Peggy Dukes—a health support worker— and Jessica, who hovered uncertainly on the fringes of the medical team.

The motorcyclist was barely more than a boy and as Ali tore open his shirt, exposing his chest, she irrelevantly noticed the smattering of freckles across his snub nose. Harvey immediately began cardiac massage while Maggie placed an oxygen mask over the boy's nose and mouth before Samara moved forward with the defibrillator.

'Stand clear!' Samara ordered before placing the pads on the boy's chest. Anxiously the staff watched the monitor for the bleep and flicker that would signify success, but none came. Again Samara attempted resuscitation, but again without success.

'I sorry,' she said at last in her broken English, 'we have lost him. Thank you, everyone, for your efforts.'

Immediately the team turned to the other patient, the girl whose condition was already being assessed by Beth and Peggy.

The girl was conscious and moaning softly, obviously in great pain from her injuries. Beth had already set up oxygen to assist with her breathing, and as Ali approached the bed Beth glanced up. 'Could you start cutting her clothes off, Ali?'

Ali nodded and beckoned Jessica forward. 'I want you to bag each piece of clothing,' she said. 'A separate bag for each item. The police may require them later for evidence.'

Taking a sharp pair of scissors, Ali carefully inserted one blade into a blood-stained tear between the girl's hip-bone and her groin and began cutting. Gradually the frayed denim fell away to reveal severe injuries to the pelvis and upper thighs. The jagged wounds were still bleeding, the blood seeping into the blue denim and dyeing it purple. Ali worked steadily and soon Jessica had placed all the girl's clothing in plastic bags.

Samara then examined the girl thoroughly, relating the injuries to Ali as she went. 'She has right-sided haemopneumothorax. I need to put in chest drain to remove blood and air from the chest cavity. I suspect fractured pelvis—I also want X-rays of neck, chest and both femurs. Blood loss is severe.'

'Her pulse is rapid and blood pressure low,' reported Beth.

'I want cross-matching,' said Samara, 'but, in the meantime, we will replace with Haemaccel. There are no head injuries so we give analgesic to reduce pain.'

'Intramuscularly?' asked Ali.

'No, intravenous,' replied Samara. 'We may have peripheral shutdown.'

'What's that?' asked Jessica.

'It means venous and arterial circulation is diminished,' explained Ali, 'or—put another way—veins and arteries aren't functioning as they should.'

The team worked methodically, setting up the Haemaccel—a synthetic blood replacement—and the analgesic, and taking blood samples for cross-matching while Samara inserted a chest drain.

Once the girl's breathing and circulation were stabilised and her pain partly controlled, attention was given to her legs which, until then, had been supported by pillows.

While Harvey maintained traction to each leg, Ali and Beth applied splints and then, as urine had not spontaneously been passed since admission, the patient was catheterised by Maggie prior to her transferral to X-Ray.

'She's the same age as me,' said Jessica as the porters wheeled the trolley out of the treatment room.

'Do you know her?' asked Ali, throwing Jessica a quick glance.

'Only by sight. I vaguely remember her from junior school.'

'And the boy?' asked Ali quietly.

'No.' Jessica shook her head and glanced across at the covered figure on the other bed. 'I didn't know him. . .' She paused. 'When will she be told?'

'When she's a little stronger,' replied Ali.

'Poor girl. . .' Jessica's voice shook. 'I don't know how I would feel if that was my boyfriend.'

'You did well there,' said Ali quickly. 'That was a particularly nasty one. They aren't all that bad.'

'I didn't really have time to think,' replied Jessica, 'and then when I did I was so interested I didn't have time to feel ill.'

'Good.' Ali smiled. 'Well, I suggest we get cleared up in here.' She glanced at her fob watch, wondering with a sudden pang what had happened to Connor. Was he still in Reception?

Almost as if she could read her thoughts, Maggie looked up from the instrument trolley as the rest of the staff left the room.

'You never told me you'd had that close a relationship with anyone.' There was a faintly accusing note in her voice, as if she found it strange that Ali hadn't thought fit to mention such an important fact in the last eighteen months.

'I was trying to forget it,' said Ali quietly.

'So, who is he?' Clearly Maggie wasn't going to be put off.

Ali sighed. 'His name is Connor Stevens.'

'And where did you meet him?'

'He was a junior doctor at the hospital where I did my training.'

'Instant attraction?' Maggie raised her eyebrows.

'Something like that,' Ali admitted.

'He's very attractive; all that dark hair and those eyes. . .so blue. . .what a combination!'

'You don't have to tell me.' Ali pulled a face as she peeled off her surgical gloves.

'So what went wrong?'

Ali shrugged. 'I suppose you could say he didn't want a long-term commitment.'

'But you lived together?' Maggie persisted.

'Oh, yes, we lived together, or rather I should say he moved in with me. He'd been thrown out of his digs at the time—too many noisy parties, I suspect. Anyway, I took pity on him. . .more fool me.' She glanced up and, catching sight of Maggie's incredulous expression, she said, 'He was pretty wild in those days, Maggie, I can tell you—drank too much, smoked too much, partied too much. You name it, Connor did it and did it to excess.'

'So he was a bad boy. . .?'

'You could say that. . .yes. . .'

'And you?'

'What do you mean—me?' Immediately Ali found herself on the defensive as she usually did when asked anything about Connor.

'Didn't you know what he was like before. . . before. . .?'

'Before I allowed him to share my flat and my bed— is that what you mean?'

'Well, yes, I suppose so.' Maggie had the grace to look a little embarrassed at being so forthright.

'Oh, yes, I guess I knew,' Ali nodded grimly. 'Why did I let him move in? I suppose I thought I could tame him. Change him, if you like.'

'And you couldn't—is that it?'

'Something like that.' Ali nodded as images of those two crazy years spent with Connor flitted across her mind.

'I bet you had fun trying.' Maggie grinned suddenly.

'We fought like cat and dog.'

'That's what I mean. I bet it was fun.'

'It was. . .traumatic. . .' she protested primly and, judging by Maggie's expression, not very convincingly.

'Oh, come on, Ali, I bet you enjoyed every minute of it—let's face it, he looked absolutely gorgeous.'

'You can't go by looks alone. . .'

'Maybe not, but they're a good place to start. So, what was he doing here?'

'I've no idea. I really can't imagine.'

'Are you saying he didn't know you worked here?' Her hands full of paper tissue, Maggie stared at her in amazement.

'That's right.' Ali wished that Maggie would shut up. Fond as she was of her, there were times when she was just too inquisitive for her own good.

'So he hadn't come in to see you, then?' Maggie looked sceptical, as if she still found it hard to believe.

'No.' Ali shook her head. 'In fact, he was surprised when he saw me.'

'So had you lost touch with each other?'

'Yes. Deliberately so. I wanted him out of my life for good.'

Maggie stared at her. 'Strong stuff,' she said after a moment then, when Ali put her head down and busied herself with the instruments that needed sterilising, she said, 'You quite obviously were very much in love with him.'

'I thought I was at the time,' Ali admitted and then shrugged. 'I guess I had a lucky escape.'

'And now he's back.' Maggie glanced at the door.

'No, he isn't,' replied Ali sharply. 'I told you, he didn't know I was here. . . It must have simply been a coincidence, that's all. Maybe he'd had an accident, or perhaps he was asking about someone else.' She tried to sound positive but she knew from her friend's expression that she wasn't convinced.

'Well, there's only one way to find out.'

'No!' she said sharply and then more calmly, 'No, Maggie. . .'

'Want me to go out first and see if he's still around?'

'No, it's OK; I'll come with you. I'm sure he will have gone by now.' She followed Maggie out of the treatment room and into Reception but the furtive glance she cast around had nothing in common with the contrived calmness of her manner. Seeing Connor again had upset her badly—far more than she had been prepared to admit to Maggie. To her relief there was no sign of him in Reception.

'Ask Chrissie,' urged Maggie at her elbow.

'No, I don't think I'll bother. . .' she began.

'Don't be silly; it'll put your mind at rest. Oh, for goodness' sake, I'll do it.'

As Maggie turned to the desk Jessica appeared from the sluice. 'I've finished cleaning up,' she said to Ali. 'What next?'

'I think it's probably lunchtime,' she said and then, in spite of herself, she found she was listening to what Maggie was saying to Chrissie.

'That's right, a tall, dark-haired chap—gorgeous-looking, blue eyes.'

'Oh, yes, him!' Chrissie's eyes lit up. 'How could I forget?'

'Was he a patient?' asked Maggie.

'I don't think so.' Chrissie shook her head.

Out of the corner of her eye Ali saw a man approach the desk, his hand wrapped in a towel.

'Can you remember what he wanted?' persisted Maggie.

Chrissie screwed up her face in concentration. 'I think he wanted to speak to Harvey,' she said.

'Harvey?' Ali frowned and as the man began unwrapping the towel she leaned forward. 'Did he say why?'

'No.' Chrissie shook her head. 'He didn't see him because Harvey was tied up with that RTA at the time.'

'What have you done to your hand?' Jessica asked the man with the towel.

'Got a fish hook embedded in my thumb,' said the man. 'Here, take a look.'

'So, did he wait?' asked Ali.

'Don't think so,' replied Chrissie. 'He certainly wasn't around when the RTA was over. Can I have your name please, sir?' She leaned across the desk.

So he'd gone, thought Ali. Well, thank God for that. She was about to move away from the desk

when she heard a thud behind her. She turned quickly
and found that Jessica had slipped to the floor in a
dead faint.

CHAPTER TWO

ALI'S house wasn't far from the hospital, in Church Close, a quiet little cluster of buildings in the mellow red brick that was so characteristic of the area. When the weather was good she chose to cycle to and from work on her ancient, upright bicycle and usually she loved her ride home, the moment when she swept into the close, dismounted, wheeled her bicycle to the rear of the house, propped it against the wall and, on entering the house, being greeted by Boy Blue, her beautiful, grey cat.

Tonight, however, she was preoccupied and Boy Blue received a somewhat absent-minded greeting even through, as she let herself into the house and picked up her post, the cat rubbed himself adoringly around her legs. Even the beauty of the tranquil May evening had been lost on her because, although she would have been loath to admit it—to Maggie or to anyone else for that matter—the sight of Connor had disturbed her tremendously.

What had he been doing in Denehurst? Could it simply have been a coincidence?

Ali had deliberately come to Denehurst because it was well off the beaten track, several miles from Winchester and from Newbury; a small town that, unless you were visiting someone, you would usually pass straight through.

Could Connor have known she was there? Was it her he had come to see? She had known, through a mutual friend, that he had tried to find her at the beginning but that had been a long time ago, long before she had

21

come to Denehurst. And he had looked surprised when
he had first caught sight of her, she had to admit that.
Chrissie had said he had asked for Harvey, but why
would he do that?

Automatically she took a tin from the fridge and
began spooning cat food into Boy Blue's bowl. Did he
know Harvey? Could it be that they were old friends?
Had she been working with Harvey all this time without
knowing that he knew Connor? She shuddered slightly
at the thought. She had never mentioned Connor to
anyone at St Mark's, not even to Maggie with whom
she had become close. She had wanted him right out
of her life; had almost wanted to pretend that she had
never known him.

But that was impossible, and she had never quite
achieved it.

With a sigh, she put the bowl of cat food on the
kitchen floor, took a carton of orange juice from the
fridge and a tumbler from the cupboard above
the worktop.

It was impossible because she knew that she would
never be able to forget Connor. As long as she lived
she would never forget him.

Pouring the orange juice and then sipping it slowly,
she wandered into her tiny sitting-room where she drew
back the curtains and, opening the French doors, stepped
outside.

The houses in the close had once belonged to the
church and all backed onto a square, walled garden. In
its centre a huge macrocarpa spread its branches over
a mossy lawn, while around the edges, behind colourful
herbaceous borders, clematis and wisteria clung to the
brick walls. In a far corner a laburnum shed its petals,
forming a golden carpet on the flagstoned path.

Most of the other residents in the close were elderly
and rarely used the garden so for Ali it had become a

refuge—a place of her own, a place to unwind and relax after a busy day at work. Still sipping her orange juice, she sat down on a bench beneath the wall, then lifted her face to the last of the day's sun. Moments later she felt a movement at her feet and, without looking, she reached down, her hand coming into contact with Boy Blue's thick fur.

'Hello, you old softie,' she said, her fingers stroking around the cat's ears and then, as he arched his back and lifted his head, moving under his chin where she gently scratched with her nails until he purred in ecstasy. 'You remember Connor, don't you? You adored him, you fickle creature.' The cat purred louder. 'I don't doubt you would welcome him back with open paws.'

With a sigh she leaned her head back against the wall and closed her eyes.

It was ironic that she had seen him again after all this time at this time of the year, because it had been May when they had first met. Exactly five years ago almost to the day, she thought ruefully, allowing her thoughts to wander. Usually she kept a tight rein on her memories because it was too easy to slip back; to remember how it had once been; to recall only the good times and to forget the others. . . To wallow in the past; to sink into depression and then find it not only difficult but almost impossible to climb out of the pit of her own making and get on with her life again.

They had met at a party.

Maybe it wouldn't do any harm to think about it. Just this once.

She shifted slightly as Boy Blue suddenly jumped onto her lap and turned round a couple of times kneading her skirt, before settling down. She wouldn't think too much. Just about their meeting. Not that she could ever forget that. Who would, after having a pint of beer spilt down their back?

'I'm most terribly sorry.'

She'd been angry at first, very angry. After all, she'd been wearing a new top, but she hadn't stayed angry for long. No one could, not faced with those incredible blue eyes.

'Here let me help you.' He'd set the glass down, gone into the house, fetched a wet cloth and proceeded to sponge the beer from her new cerise-coloured top. She even remembered the colour of the top, for heaven's sake! Remembered every detail of that meeting, come to that. And most of what came afterwards.

The party, or rather barbeque, had been in the garden of a house shared by several medical students from the teaching hospital where Ali was doing her training.

'I don't believe we've met,' he said, as his fingers brushed the skin between her shoulder-blades.

'No,' she admitted, 'I don't believe we have. I'm Ali McKenzie—I'm in my second year RGN.'

'Connor Stevens—junior houseman. Let me get another drink and we'll talk. . . What are you drinking?' His accent was as devastating as his eyes.

'White wine.'

'Right.' He took her glass and began shouldering his way through the crowd in the garden.

It had been a night just like this, she thought. . .warm, not a breath of wind, sunshine lingering before it sank into shadow, seductive. . . She should have known, really. But how could she? She'd been young then, fresh and eager, vulnerable, and really rather naïve.

He'd come back astonishingly quickly, given the number of people who thronged the house and garden, almost as if he was afraid that she would disappear.

'Are you in digs or in the nurses' home?' he asked as he handed her her wine.

'The nurses' home,' she replied, noticing again the blue of his eyes and the impossibly dark fringe of lashes that surrounded them. 'But not for long.'

'Really?' He raised his glass. 'Cheers.'

'Cheers.' She smiled. 'I'm moving into my own place. It's only small, but at least it'll be mine. What about you? Are you in hospital accommodation?'

'No,' he shook his head and grinned, 'I'm in digs. . . at the moment.'

'What do you mean—at the moment?'

'My landlady and I don't quite see eye to eye.'

He didn't elaborate further but she caught the gleam of amusement in his eyes, thought it infectious and found herself smiling back. Shortly after that they had been caught up in a group of other students but Ali found herself watching him, studying him, when she knew he wasn't looking.

There was something about him that fascinated her and it wasn't only the unusual combination of his dark hair and bright blue eyes, devastating as that was. No, it also had something to do with his easy, almost lazy movements and the way he dressed—the torn denims, which would have looked scruffy on anyone else but which on him merely looked casual, and the black T-shirt under an open-necked white shirt, its cuffs turned back almost to the elbow.

It was something to do with the way he wore his dark hair unfashionably long while everyone else's was short and last, but by no means least, there was the devastating charm of his southern Irish accent. It all helped to make him different. The one who stood out from the crowd.

Once, as if he sensed her eyes on him, he turned suddenly, giving her no chance to look away, and as their eyes met she instinctively knew in that instant that he was going to play an important part in her life.

He made his way back to her side then and didn't leave it again. They talked all night and although Ali found they had little or nothing in common she was still fascinated.

'So, how come a hard-up student nurse can afford her own place?' he asked much later as they swayed together to the strains of a saxophone on the small patio.

'I'm lucky,' she replied. 'My grandmother has put some money in trust for me. The interest will pay my rent.'

'Wish I had a grandmother like that,' he murmured against her hair.

'She was a nurse in her younger days,' laughed Ali. 'She remembered. Nurses' homes were like prisons in those days.'

'Not a lot better now,' he muttered.

When at last the first edges of dawn were touching the garden and the neighbours had threatened for the umpteenth time to call the police, the party broke up and Connor asked if he could see her again.

As she recalled the moment the telephone suddenly rang in the house behind her, and Boy Blue stirred. Ali lifted her head, then gently eased the cat from her lap and stood up. Maybe, she thought as she went back into the house, that was where she had made her first mistake; maybe that was when she should have said no; said she didn't want to see him again. Maybe at that point she could have done it because later—only a short time later—it had been impossible because by then she had been well and truly hooked.

It was Maggie on the phone.

'I was worried about you,' she said.

'Why?'

'I don't know really... You seemed...seemed somehow...oh, I don't know...just different. It was seeing that guy. Wasn't it? That Connor?'

'Well, yes, I suppose it did throw me a bit,' Ali admitted.

'Well, it would. After all, it isn't every day you see someone you've actually lived with, is it?'

'No, Maggie,' she said patiently.

'I mean, living with someone is really a bit like being married to them, isn't it?'

'Yes, it is. In fact, it's a lot like being married to someone.'

'What?' said Maggie. 'Oh, yes, yes, I agree. Anyway, I was worried about you. Do you want me to come over?'

'No, no, Maggie,' she said quickly. 'Really, I'm fine. It just threw me a bit, that's all. I couldn't think what he was doing in Denehurst.'

'Well, no, exactly.' Maggie paused. 'I knew that's what you were worried about. . .so I had a word with Harvey.'

'You did what?' Ali's hand instinctively tightened round the receiver.

'I had a word with Harvey after you'd gone. You know Chrissie said that this. . . Connor was looking for Harvey. . . Ali, are you still there?'

'Yes.' She took a deep breath, holding onto her temper with difficulty. 'So what did Harvey say?'

'Well, that was the strange part. Said he'd never heard of anyone called Connor Stevens. . .'

'Maybe someone simply asked him. . . Connor, I mean. . .' she swallowed; it was hard even saying his name again '. . .to look Harvey up.'

'Yes, maybe.' Maggie sounded doubtful. 'Well, whatever it was, we'll probably never know. He didn't come back. No doubt he's miles away by now.'

'Hopefully, yes.'

'You're very bitter, aren't you, Ali?'

'No, not bitter exactly, just extremely thankful he's out of my life for good.'

'You didn't mind. . .' Maggie suddenly sounded

anxious '. . .my asking Harvey? You see, I was only concerned about you.'

'I know, Maggie, it's OK; don't give it another thought.'

'Are you absolutely sure you don't want me to come round? I could, you know. . .'

'No, Maggie, honestly. I'm fine, really I am.'

'All right. I'll see you tomorrow, then.'

'Bye, Maggie.' Ali replaced the receiver. Just for one moment there she had been angry with Maggie—that old temper of hers had flared but really, when she thought about it, she knew what Maggie had said was the truth. She had only been concerned about her and had been trying to help. And besides, she thought as Boy Blue stalked back into the house and she closed the French doors, what did it matter? As Maggie had said, Connor was probably miles away by now.

A pang shot through her. Maybe it would have been nice to have talked to him for a little while.

Slowly she wandered up the stairs to her bedroom and pushed open the door. The last of the afternoon sunshine streamed through the window and across the bed. He had looked exactly the same to her. Would she have looked the same to him?

Crossing the room, she paused in front of the dressing-table then, bending down, she peered curiously in the mirror. Had she changed in the last three years? Her hair was different but he'd noticed that immediately— surprisingly had said he liked it short—but what about the rest of her?

She sank down onto the stool and began scrutinising her features. Her mouth still looked too wide for the rest of her face but Connor had never seemed to notice that, her jaw was squarish where she would have loved a little pointed chin, her skin was still clear and healthy and her eyes—probably her best feature—

were green, thick-lashed beneath dark brows.

He'd loved her eyes—said they tantalised him, that she must have had a witch as one of her ancestors. Had he remembered saying that when he'd seen her today?

Abruptly she stood up. She mustn't think of things like that—it wouldn't do any good. Turning away from the dressing-table, she unbuttoned the blouse she wore for work, then unzipped her skirt and stepped out of it. Maybe a long, leisurely bath would banish these disconcerting thoughts of Connor. Unhooking her bra and peeling off her briefs, she opened the wardrobe door to get her robe. She was about to shut the door when she caught sight of her naked figure in the full-length mirror on the inside of the door and again the critical self-appraisal began.

If her face hadn't changed, what about her figure?

She was still slim—maybe a little too thin? But her breasts were still taut and nicely rounded. Slowly she brought her hands up and cupped them, then turned sideways. Her hip-bones protruded slightly but her stomach was gently curved. She'd protested once that she was getting fat and Connor had laughed at her, then teased her about it sometimes when they'd made love.

What would he think of her now? He used to say that she was beautiful—would he still think so? Would she still arouse and excite him so much that he would lose all control the way he used to?

Suddenly, as she stared at her reflection, she was aware that an almost forgotten but strangely familiar ache had started somewhere deep inside her body. An ache she had not experienced since Connor had gone out of her life. Desperately her hands tightened over her breasts and a sob caught in her throat.

She mustn't think of that now. What did it matter if she had changed? Connor would never know. Today had simply been one of those chance meetings. Ships passing in the night. A never-to-be repeated encounter.

Abruptly she turned away from the mirror. She had to forget it. Mustn't allow herself to start thinking about the past. It only upset her.

It must have been like being married, Maggie had said. And that is exactly what it had been like. No one had warned her of that at the time. If she had only known. . .

She spent a troubled night, her sleep fitful and intermingled with haunting dreams which, when she awakened, she had trouble recalling but which she had the uneasy feeling had all been about Connor.

When she got to work she found Jessica waiting for her.

'I'm sorry about yesterday.' The girl looked upset, with dark circles beneath her blue eyes as if she, too, had spent a sleepless night.

'Yesterday?' For one moment Ali couldn't think what she was referring to.

'Yes, fainting like that. I felt such a fool.'

'Oh, that,' said Ali with a dismissive little gesture. 'Don't think anything of it. It happens to all of us from time to time.'

'I thought I was getting better,' said Jessica miserably. 'I didn't bat an eyelid over all that blood with the RTA, then a man with a fish hook and I keel over! Honestly, what a wimp!'

'It's the most unexpected things that get to you, Jessica.'

'I know.' The girl shuddered. 'I think it was just the thought of a hook embedded in that man's thumb and then I remembered hearing something someone once said about a fish hook having to be pushed on through if it's stuck in the flesh and, well, the thought of that just finished me off.'

'We all have something that gets to us,' said Ali.

'Really?' Jessica looked as if she didn't believe her.

'Yes,' Ali nodded. 'Want to know what it is with me?'

Jessica nodded, her eyes rounding almost fearfully as if she wondered what she was about to hear.

'Well, before I worked here I did a spell in general theatre and saw practically every op' there is—appendectomies, colostomies, gall bladders removed, lumps removed—you name it, I saw it.'

'Oh, gosh. . .!'

'But do you know the thing that makes me almost pass out?'

'No. . . What?'

'Watching someone have a toenail removed.'

'Oh!'

They were both still laughing when they reached Reception. 'So don't worry about it,' said Ali firmly. 'You look as if it gave you a sleepless night.'

'Yes, well, I suppose it did,' muttered Jessica, 'but it wasn't only that. I'm having problems with my boyfriend at the moment as well. . .'

'Ah, well, that's guaranteed to give anyone a sleepless night,' observed Ali drily. 'Right, Harvey,' she said as they approached the nurses' station, 'what have you got for us?'

The charge nurse looked up from the desk at the nurses' station, pushed back the lock of hair that always flopped over his forehead and peered at them both over the top of his glasses. 'What would you like?' he said with a sigh. 'You could probably take your pick this morning—name it and it's here.'

'Oh dear, like that, is it?' said Ali, pulling a face. 'Well, no one can say you aren't getting a thorough initiation,' she said to Jessica. 'What's the staff situation like?' She glanced at the blackboard on the wall, then turned back to Harvey.

'Like it always is—desperately short,' he replied grimly. 'I'm meeting the managers later today to plead our case once again. The only bright spot as far as I can see is that they've at last appointed another CO to help relieve Samara.'

'Thank God for that,' said Ali. 'It's not before time. I was getting worried about Samara;' she was beginning to look absolutely dead beat. The hours she's been doing have been horrendous.'

'Exactly.' Harvey also glanced at the board. 'Right, Ali, take Jessica and go to Cubicle Three. A lady's had a fall in the street. Has been brought in by ambulance. Get details, history and do an assessment.'

'OK. Come on, Jessica,' said Ali.

They left the nurses' station and in the corridor Ali pulled back the curtains around Cubicle Three.

An elderly lady was lying on the bed and a faint smell of eau-de-cologne hung in the air.

Irene Bridges, a support worker, was talking to the patient. She looked up and smiled at Ali and Jessica. 'Hello,' she said, 'this is Mrs Burrows. She was on her way to the shops when she had a fall. Someone called for an ambulance and she was brought here. I'll leave her in your hands.'

'Hello, Mrs Burrows.' Ali nodded at Irene who left the cubicle. 'Can you remember what happened to you?'

Mrs Burrows's face was pale, her mouth twisted with pain. She had a gash on her forehead and a cut on the bridge of her nose. 'I fell,' she said. 'Over a paving stone, I think; I'm not really sure. It all happened so quickly. I'm sorry to be such a nuisance.'

'You're not a nuisance, Mrs Burrows,' said Ali firmly. 'Now, I want you to tell me where it hurts.'

'My leg. . .I couldn't get up. . . That's why they called an ambulance. But I think I'm all right now, dear. Do you think I could go home now?'

'I think first we'd better get a doctor to have a look at that leg and maybe have a few X-rays done just to make sure you haven't broken anything,' said Ali.

'Oh, I don't think that will be necessary.' Mrs Burrows began to struggle to get up. 'I really must be going now—my sister will be wondering where I've got to.'

'Do you live with your sister, Mrs Burrows?' asked Ali.

'Oh, no, dear. I live alone, but I keep an eye on my sister and do her shopping for her. She's getting on a bit, you see. She'll be eighty-five in August.'

'Really?' Ali smiled. 'And how old are you?'

'Oh, I'm only eighty-one,' replied Mrs Burrows, and as she struggled again to get up she gave a sudden cry of pain and fell back against the pillows.

'That leg is very painful, isn't it?' said Jessica, taking hold of the old lady's hand.

'Yes, dear.' Mrs Burrows bit her lip. 'It is rather.'

'So we've got to do something about it, haven't we?' said Ali gently.

'Yes, I suppose so.' She nodded and sighed.

'First of all I want Jessica to take your pulse, then I'm going to check your blood pressure. After that, we will help you to get undressed so we can make sure you don't have any other injuries.'

'But what about my sister. . .?'

'Is she on the telephone?' asked Ali as she began to set up a sphygmomanometer.

'Yes. . .but she gets very confused. She would worry more if someone phoned and said I'd had an accident.'

'In that case, is there a neighbour we could phone who could go round and explain, or maybe you would prefer that we arrange for a social worker to call and reassure her?'

Mrs Burrows looked agitated for a moment, then

her face cleared. 'There's Mrs Reed,' she said, 'her next-door neighbour. You could phone her; she'd go round and see Cissy.'

'Very well. Jessica can organise that, then when you've had your X-rays and know what is happening perhaps you would like to phone your sister yourself.'

'Oh, yes.' Mrs Burrows looked relieved. 'That might help to put her mind at rest.'

The next half-hour was busy as Ali carried out the required observations and Jessica made the necessary arrangements. Then, when Mrs Burrows was undressed and comfortable in a hospital gown with her injured leg supported by pillows, Ali sent Jessica to the nurses' station to see if Samara was available to carry out an examination.

'Do you think I could have a cup of tea, dear?' the old lady asked as Ali was tidying the cubicle and folding her clothes.

'I'm sorry, that's the one thing I can't let you have. Not until the doctor has seen you,' replied Ali.

'What's he like—the doctor?' asked Mrs Burrows after a moment. 'One of these young lads, I suppose, like they all are these days.'

'Actually, it's a lady,' said Ali with a smile. 'And she's very nice.' As she spoke there was the sound of footsteps outside. 'Ah,' she added, 'it sounds like she's here now.'

The curtain was drawn back just far enough to reveal Jessica's face. Ali noticed that she looked a little anxious.

'What is it, Jessica?' she asked. 'Is Samara with you?'

'No,' Jessica said, 'it isn't. . .' she trailed off as the curtain was whisked aside.

Ali glanced up, fully expecting to see Samara, but instead it was Connor Stevens who strolled into the cubicle.

CHAPTER THREE

'GOOD morning, Staff Nurse McKenzie.' The blue eyes met hers without a flicker before his gaze moved smoothly to Mrs Burrows. 'Good morning,' he said. 'I understand you've had a fall and hurt your leg. Perhaps you'd let me take a look.'

Mrs Burrows looked startled. 'You said it would be a lady doctor,' she said to Ali, her tone faintly accusing.

'That is what I thought,' muttered Ali. Mechanically she moved forward and removed the white cellular blanket covering Mrs Burrows's legs but her mind was racing. What was he doing here, for heaven's sake?

As if oblivious to the turmoil he had created, Connor stood looking down at Mrs Burrows. 'I'm sorry if I'm a disappointment,' he said.

'Well, I had been given to understand it would be a lady,' murmured Mrs Burrows.

'I'm afraid Dr Rahjid isn't on duty this morning, but I promise I can be very, very gentle.' He smiled, the smile Ali remembered so well—the smile guaranteed to charm a woman, any woman, whether she was eighteen or eighty.

Mrs Burrows smiled back. 'Very well,' she said and lay back on her pillows.

Ali sighed and glanced at Jessica and saw that she too was smiling as she gazed in open admiration at Connor Stevens. Her mind still in chaos, she watched as he examined the patient, her eyes drawn involuntarily to the movements of his hands. She had so loved those hands once. Strong, capable and beautifully shaped, the palms broad and the fingers long but squared at the

35

tips. How many times in the past had they moved over her body, arousing her to undreamed-of heights of desire. . .? Angrily she checked herself. What in the world was she doing, allowing herself to think of such things?

'I think, Mrs Burrows, we need to get a couple of X-rays or so. . . Maybe Nurse can arrange that. . .' He glanced up at Jessica but it was Ali who intervened.

'I'll see to that,' she said crisply. 'You stay here, Jessica.' She was aware of Connor's look of surprise, but she didn't care. She had to get out of the cubicle which suddenly had grown very claustrophobic. She needed also to get away from him. From Connor, from his presence, from the enforced nearness of him which had badly shaken her. But, most of all, she needed to know what he was doing there in the cubicle, so calmly treating her patient.

She strode out into Reception past the nurses' station, only vaguely aware of Maggie's look of concern as she glanced up from behind the desk, and, barely pausing to knock on Harvey's door, she swept into his office.

The charge nurse looked up from the staff rota he was working on. 'Ali. . .? What is it. . .?' he asked in surprise.

'What's he doing here?' she demanded.

'Who?' Harvey frowned.

'Him.' She jerked her thumb over her shoulder. 'That man. Connor Stevens.'

'Oh.' Harvey's face cleared a little. He had obviously thought that they had a problem patient in Reception. 'Him.'

'What's he doing here, Harvey?' Ali repeated. 'I want to know.'

'He's the new casualty officer.'

'What?' She stared at him, hardly able to believe what she was hearing.

'Yes, he's the relief I requested for Samara. . . I thought you would be pleased, Ali.' Harvey suddenly looked curious. 'You were always saying Samara worked too hard, that she needed some help.'

'I know,' Ali snapped. 'Samara does need help. . . but not him! Not Connor Stevens!'

'I don't understand.' Harvey frowned. 'What's wrong with him? He seemed a nice enough chap to me. . .'

'You said you didn't know him,' she accused.

'What?' He looked bewildered, as if the whole incident was getting too much for him.

'Yesterday he called to see you.'

'Apparently so. Yes, he did.'

'And you told Chrissie you'd never heard of him.'

'That's perfectly true. I hadn't. Not then. I merely knew that a new CO had been appointed. But I hadn't been told his name. When Chrissie told me a Connor Stevens had called in to see me the name meant nothing. If she had said the new CO had been in, I would have known what she meant. Look, Ali, what is all this. . .? I don't understand.'

'It's quite simple, Harvey.' Ali drew herself up, straightening her shoulders. 'If Connor Stevens is your new CO, then you'd better start looking for a new staff nurse.'

'What. . .?' Harvey's eyes narrowed and he leaned back in his chair. 'What do you mean, Ali?'

'Exactly what I say. If he stays, then I go.'

'But why? I still don't understand.'

'It's simple. I won't work in the same department as him. . . I'm sorry, Harvey, but there it is.' Turning abruptly, she tugged open the door and collided with someone who was about to enter. 'I'm sorry,' she muttered then, glancing up, realised to her dismay that it was Connor.

'Oh, Dr Stevens,' said Harvey, 'we were just discussing your appointment. . .'

Not waiting to hear more, Ali fled from the office, not stopping until she reached the comparative sanctuary of the nurses' rest-room where she locked herself in the loo. Her heart was hammering in her chest as she leaned against the door, struggling to regain her composure. It couldn't be true. He couldn't have come here to Denehurst, of all places. Damn him! Oh, damn him! Furiously she clenched her fists. She had been happy here. Had just started, after all this time, to get her life back together.

Now he was back, and it was all threatened again.

'Ali, are you in there?' There came an urgent tap on the door and she recognised Maggie's voice.

'Yes,' she mumbled.

'Are you all right? Is there anything I can do?'

'No. I'm OK. I'll be out in a minute.' She leaned over the wash basin and turned on the tap. She knew Maggie wouldn't go until she opened the door. She filled the basin then cupping her hands filled them with water and splashed it over her face. The shock of the cold water seemed to restore her reason, as a slap did when administered for hysteria. Taking a paper towel, she carefully blotted her face and wiped her hands before dropping the towel in the waste bin. By the time she opened the door and faced an anxious Maggie she was feeling calmer.

'Ali, I'm sorry—it's him, isn't it? The new CO?'

'You knew?' Ali raised her eyebrows.

'Only just. I had no time to warn you. . .I'm sorry. I know what a shock it must have been for you.'

Ali shrugged. 'Yes, it was.'

'Well, maybe it might not be so bad as you might think.'

'What do you mean?' Calmly she turned to Maggie.

'Working with him. You must be feeling apprehensive about it. . .but it might not be so bad. He seemed so nice. . .all the others have said so.'

'Good for them,' replied Ali. 'If you are going to be working with someone it's usually better if you actually like them.'

'Oh.' Maggie threw her an uncertain look. 'Well, I'm glad you feel that way, Ali. . . I was afraid. . .'

'Oh, I didn't mean myself,' said Ali smoothly.

'You didn't?' There was a decided note of bewilderment in Maggie's voice now.

'No. Because I shan't be here.'

'Whatever do you mean?'

'Exactly what I say,' replied Ali, struggling now to stay calm and to fight the tide of emotion that was beginning to rise again inside her and which this time she was afraid would totally overwhelm her. 'I told Harvey if Connor Stevens stays, then I go.'

'Oh, Ali!' Dismay filled Maggie's eyes. 'You don't mean that.'

'Don't I?' retorted Ali. 'Just watch me.'

'But this is crazy. Why should you go, for God's sake?' cried Maggie. 'You love it here. You love your job; you have a lovely home. You have friends. Are you saying you would be prepared to give all that up just because of him. . .this man?'

Ali didn't reply. Maggie stared at her for a moment, then carried on. 'I wouldn't give any man the satisfaction of knowing that he had got to me that much.'

'You don't understand,' muttered Ali at last.

'I probably understand better than you think,' said Maggie. 'You say you lived with him?'

'Yes,' mumbled Ali.

'For two years?'

She nodded.

'And it didn't work out? Well, that really isn't any big deal—not these days, Ali.'

'It was to me.' Ali looked up sharply. 'I loved him, damn it. I thought that by living together we were making a statement, a commitment to each other.'

'So what went wrong?' asked Maggie curiously.

'He needed to grow up.'

'Maybe he has now,' said Maggie quietly.

'I don't intend finding out,' retorted Ali sharply. 'He damn near destroyed me last time. I have no intention of letting him have a second try.'

At that moment there came a hammering on the door. 'Are we running an accident and emergency department here or not?' Harvey shouted through the door.

'Sorry, Harvey,' called Maggie, 'we'll be right with you. Come on, Ali,' she said. 'You can't let Harvey down in the middle of a shift.'

'No. Maybe I can't,' agreed Ali tightly. 'But I mean what I say. I shall resign if Connor Stevens stays.'

'Oh, Ali!' Helplessly Maggie stared at her.

'I'm sorry, Maggie, but it's quite simple. I just don't want to be where he is.'

Reception was in chaos by the time Ali and Maggie returned. The rows of chairs were packed with patients waiting for attention. Someone was repeatedly pressing the bell on the reception desk. Chrissie was on the telephone and Di, the other duty receptionist, was trying to restrain a small boy whose finger was stuck in a piece of pipe and who was screaming his head off. Two ambulances had apparently just arrived at the emergency entrance. A white-faced Jessica was trying to calm a woman who appeared to be having hysterics, and someone else was vomiting noisily in the corner.

'Oh, my God!' muttered Maggie, 'get a load of this lot. We turn our backs for five minutes and the whole show falls apart.'

As Ali glanced round, trying to ascertain where her priorities should be, Connor suddenly appeared from the nurses' station. His gaze immediately met hers, the expression in his blue eyes quizzical yet faintly amused. Ali quickly transferred her gaze to Harvey, who had followed him out of the station.

'Oh, good—' the sarcasm in Harvey's voice was only barely concealed '—you two have decided to honour us with your presence. Maggie, see to this child; Ali, cubicles, please.

Ignoring Connor, Ali followed Harvey to the nurses' station. 'What's happened to Mrs Burrows?' she asked.

'She's still in X-Ray,' replied Harvey, studying the blackboard that gave details of admissions. 'Cubicle Five, Ali. Peggy's in there with a young man who's fallen from the top of the wall bars in the gym at his school. Do an assessment, please, then I'll send Dr Stevens to have a look at him.'

With a sigh Ali turned away. There was going to be no avoiding Connor, at least for the time being. She found Peggy, a support worker, in Cubicle Five with a very frightened eight-year-old boy.

'Hi, Ali.' Peggy looked up from unlacing the boy's trainers. 'This is Ben—he's had rather a nasty fall.'

'Is me mum coming?' Tears trickled slowly down the boy's cheeks.

'Hello, Ben.' Ali smiled and glanced at Peggy before she attempted to answer his question, simple as it seemed.

'Apparently his father is on his way,' said Peggy.

'I want me mum.' The boy gave a sudden loud sob.

'Where is your mum, Ben?' asked Ali gently as she began to ease off his jacket.

'At work.' He sniffed.

'Maybe she can't get here for the moment if she's at work,' suggested Ali.

'He won't tell her,' said Ben sullenly after a moment.

'Who won't tell her?' asked Ali, suddenly noticing a large lump on the side of the boy's head which seemed to grow even as she watched it.

'Me dad,' muttered Ben.

Ali caught Peggy's eye and the mutual unspoken agreement that flashed between them was that the subject should be changed. 'Did you fall from the very top of the bars, Ben?' she asked.

'Yep,' the boy nodded and for one moment looked proud. 'First time I got to the top,' he added.

'So tell me where it hurts,' said Ali.

'Here.' Ben pointed to his head. 'And here.' He touched his right shoulder and winced.

'I see. Anywhere else?' asked Ali.

'No.' The boy shook his head. 'I don't think so.'

'You couldn't walk, Ben,' said Peggy. 'When you came in the ambulance man carried you, didn't he?'

'Yes. . .' Ben nodded. 'I was dizzy.'

As Ali eased his sock off, immediately she saw that his right ankle was swollen. 'Does this hurt, Ben?' she asked.

'Oh, yes.' He looked surprised. 'Yes, it does.'

At that moment Jessica put her head through the curtains. 'Mr Taylor, Ben's father, is here,' she said.

'Very well, ask him to come in,' said Ali, looking up.

A moment later an anxious-looking man entered the cubicle. 'Ben?' he said, his gaze darting to his son, 'are you all right?'

'Is Mum with you?' asked Ben, ignoring his father's question.

'No.' The man shook his head and, standing beside the bed, took his son's hand. 'That was a silly thing to do—falling off the bars, wasn't it?'

'I slipped,' said Ben.

'Here's the doctor,' said Peggy as Connor appeared.

'He'll want to examine Ben. Do you want to wait outside, Mr Taylor?'

'I'd rather stay.' The man looked even more anxious than before.

'Of course you can,' said Connor easily as Peggy extricated herself from the cubicle which was becoming decidedly crowded, leaving Ali to give the assessment.

'So, what have you been up to, old man?' asked Connor looking down at Ben.

'Fell off the wall bars,' said Ben, then added, 'I want Mum.'

'What do we have, Staff Nurse?' asked Connor, half turning towards Ali.

'Raised pulse, dizziness, a lump on his head, pain in right shoulder and swelling to right ankle,' said Ali crisply.

'Right, well, we'd better take a look, hadn't we?' said Connor.

'Will Mum come?' asked Ben anxiously as Connor began to examine him.

'I don't know,' replied Connor, glancing at Mr Taylor. 'Is that likely?' he asked.

The man shook his head. 'My wife and I are separated,' he mumbled. 'Ben lives with me.'

'Has his mother been told?' asked Connor.

Again Mr Taylor shook his head.

'Don't you think it might be a good idea if she was told?'

'Why?' The man immediately looked alarmed. 'Is it serious?'

'I shouldn't think so for one moment,' said Connor calmly, 'but that wasn't the point I was making. Don't you think the boy's mother would want to be here?'

'Dad. . .?' asked Ben when Mr Taylor didn't immediately reply.

'Ben obviously wants his mum here,' said Ali quietly.

'Would you like me to phone her place of work?'

'Yes, and that means he'd bring her,' muttered Mr Taylor.

'Who?' asked Connor as he began examining Ben's legs, bending each in turn at the knee.

'Him. Roger. Her boyfriend.' There was no disguising the bitterness in the man's voice. 'He's the manager at the supermarket where she works,' he explained abruptly when neither Ali or Connor spoke. 'He's a right little prat; we don't want him here.'

Carefully Connor tested Ben's reflexes.

'I want Mum,' Ben said again then, twisting his head so that he could see his father over Connor's shoulder, he added, 'Roger's not that bad, Dad. He was dead good when I went to see them last weekend—he let me choose what video I wanted.'

Ali exchanged a glance with Connor and as he straightened up from examining Ben Mr Taylor said, 'So what's the verdict, Doctor?'

'I don't think there's too much damage done,' Connor replied. 'I think we'll have that ankle X-rayed just to make sure he hasn't cracked the bone. He will have bruising to his shoulder, and he may have a little concussion from the blow to his head.'

'Concussion? That's serious, isn't it?' Mr Taylor sounded worried.

'Not necessarily,' replied Connor. 'It's important not to let him go to sleep for a while, but he'll be here anyway until his X-ray is done so we'll keep an eye on him for a bit.'

'What about that lump on his head?'

'That'll go down in time,' replied Connor and, looking at Ben again, he said, 'You might have a headache in the morning, Ben, and maybe even a black eye.'

'My friend, Josh, had a black eye,' said Ben and

sounded quite excited at the prospect of the same thing happening to him.

'So there's nothing else we should do then, Doctor?'

'No.' Connor had been about to go out of the cubicle, but he paused and looked back at Ben. 'Apart from getting his mum, of course,' he added.

'Do you have the number, Mr Taylor?' asked Ali as Connor gave a brief nod then disappeared outside.

'Not off-hand,' he mumbled, 'but it's Asco, the big supermarket outside town.'

'I'll go and phone,' said Ali. 'What's your mum's Christian name, Ben?'

'Sandra,' the boy replied happily.

Ali stepped outside the cubicle and was about to draw the curtains when she caught sight of Mr Taylor's miserable expression. 'Don't worry,' she said, touching his shoulder, 'Ben's mother can come in on her own to see him.'

'But he'll bring her in in his car,' muttered Mr Taylor.

'Then he can wait in Reception,' replied Ali firmly. Although her first duty was to Ben and she also felt a certain sympathy towards his mother, who was ignorant of what had happened, she suddenly felt very sorry for his father and the situation he was in.

She drew the curtains and returned quickly to the nurses' station where she phoned the supermarket and, after a short delay, was able to speak to Ben's mother. The woman was understandably upset, in spite of Ali's assurances that Ben wasn't badly hurt, and said that she would come to the hospital immediately.

Ali was just replacing the receiver when a voice at her elbow said, 'Everything all right?'

She stiffened and, without turning round, said lightly, 'Yes, fine, thanks. Mrs Taylor is on her way in.'

'Minus the boyfriend?'

'I have no idea, but we'll deal with that when she

arrives. We're well used to these difficult situations.'

'I'm sure you are,' he replied smoothly, then he paused and said, 'Speaking of difficult situations, I gather we could find ourselves in the midst of one.'

'I don't know what you mean,' replied Ali, wishing that he wouldn't stand so close to her. He was so close that she could smell his aftershave. It was not the one he used to use, but another, slightly musky, unfamiliar one, but even more disconcerting was the underlying scent of him—the male scent which was only too familiar. She was unable to move away because he had her trapped in a corner of the station.

'You don't?' He sounded genuinely surprised. 'I understood from Harvey that you had some sort of problem over working with me. May I ask why?'

She gasped at his audacity and spun round to face him, only to be further disconcerted by the amusement lurking in his eyes. 'Oh, for God's sake, Connor!' she snapped. 'As if you didn't know!'

'I'm sorry—' he spread his hands apologetically '—but that's exactly it. I'm afraid I don't know.'

She stared at him incredulously. 'I don't know how you can stand there and say that after all that happened.'

'After all what that happened?' He frowned, a mystified smile playing around the corners of his mouth. In spite of herself, Ali found that she was staring at his mouth. . .the curved upper lip, the fuller, sensual lower lip. . . Hastily she looked away.

'I don't have time to play silly guessing games, Connor,' she said sharply, trying to edge past him. 'There's work to be done.'

'So you're saying there isn't a problem; that we can work together quite amicably?' He raised one eyebrow.

'I'm not say anything of the sort,' she snapped.

'I don't understand.' The dark brows drew into a frown but the quizzical amusement was still there in the depths of those incredible blue eyes.

'It's quite simple,' she said, looking squarely at him for the first time as he continued to stand his ground barring her path, 'I don't want to work with you and I don't intend working with you.'

'Then what. . .?' The amusement faded from his eyes and was replaced by a glint that would turn to anger. She'd seen that before, too.

She swallowed. 'I shall hand in my notice and look for another job.'

'In another hospital? You'd move away?'

'If I have to. If I can't find anything immediately, I shall ask for a temporary transfer to another department.'

'You would do that? Go to those lengths?'

'Yes, Connor, I would,' she said levelly.

'I see,' he said quietly. 'I had no idea you felt so strongly.'

He did move aside then to allow her to pass, but as she did so she felt a sharp pang as she caught sight of the pain in his eyes.

CHAPTER FOUR

'MRS BURROWS had a fractured femur.' Harvey glanced up from his desk. It was much later and Ali was about to go off duty. 'She's gone up to Orthopaedics,' he added.

'Poor old soul,' said Ali. 'She'll be worrying about her sister.'

'That's all in hand,' said Harvey. 'Mrs Burrows has spoken to her on the phone and the neighbour is going to look out for her. If there are any further problems Social Services will step in.'

'Any more news on Ben Taylor?' For the past couple of hours Ali had been in the treatment rooms dealing first with a pedestrian who had been run over by a transit van and then with a toddler who had inhaled a bead.

Harvey glanced at the blackboard. 'He came back from X-Ray—there were no breaks. Mild concussion. He's gone home now.'

'Did his mother come?' asked Ali curiously.

Harvey nodded. 'Yes, complete with boyfriend in tow—a mild, inoffensive little man not a patch on Ben's father. We had no problem at all persuading him to wait in Reception. Makes you wonder, doesn't it?'

'It certainly does.' Ali nodded. 'Still, ours is not to reason why. Who knows what goes on in any marriage?'

'True.' Harvey paused, picked up a folder and, opening a metal filing cabinet, found the correct section and filed it. 'You off now?' he asked, looking round after a moment and finding Ali still there.

'More or less.' She hesitated, then said, 'I meant what I said, Harvey, about not working with Connor Stevens. . . You see, I—'

'Ali,' Harvey cut her short.

'Yes?' She paused in mid-sentence.

'Don't say any more now.'

'But I mean it.'

'I know you do,' Harvey said gently, 'but I want you to go home and sleep on it. We'll discuss it again tomorrow.'

'I won't change my mind. I know him too well and I don't want to work with him again.'

'Fine.' Harvey shrugged. 'We'll discuss it tomorrow. Now, if you'll excuse me, Ali, I have a meeting upstairs with the powers that be.'

It was a dismissal and she knew it. With a sigh she turned away. She had been hoping to get things sorted out that day—at least between herself and Harvey— but it seemed that wasn't going to happen. She suspected that he was refusing to take her seriously; thought she was over-reacting and that after a night's sleep she would change her mind.

Well, he was in for a shock, she told herself grimly as she made her way to the nurses' staff-room. Kind as he might be Harvey knew nothing of her personal life or of her background but, if need be, she would tell him and then he might realise that she was deadly serious in her intentions.

Wearily she pulled off her cap and shook out her hair before unbuttoning her uniform. As she was pulling on a baggy, cotton jumper over a pair of leggings Jessica came into the room behind her. The girl looked more tired than ever.

'Ready for home?' Ali smiled and the girl managed a weary smile in response.

'Yes, I had no idea it would be so frantic all the time,' she said as she unbuttoned her uniform and stepped out of it.

'Some days are worse than others. Today's been

pretty hectic, though, I must admit,' said Ali. 'You've done well, Jessica.'

'Thanks.' The girl flushed slightly at the praise and pulled on a white T-shirt with a frog motif on the front.

Watching her, Ali remembered something she had said that morning. 'You mentioned boyfriend trouble earlier.' she said, throwing the girl a quick glance. 'Anything I can do to help?'

'I don't think so—thanks, anyway.' Jessica shrugged. 'We had a massive row last night. He wants me to move in with him. . .'

'And you don't want to?' asked Ali gently.

'I don't think I'm ready for that yet. . .'

'Then don't do it,' said Ali. 'It's as simple as that.'

Jessica looked at her curiously. 'All my friends say I should—because I won't know unless I do.'

'Presumably your friends live with their boyfriends?' asked Ali.

'Most of them, yes,' admitted Jessica, scraping her dark hair back into a ponytail and securing it with a frilly band.

'So where are you living at the moment?' asked Ali, thinking again how the girl reminded her of herself and of how she had been during her early student days.

'In the nurses' home,' Jessica replied, quickly adding, 'I lived at home with my parents before that.'

'What would they think about you moving in with your boyfriend?'

'They wouldn't interfere. . .' She hesitated.

'But. . .?'

The girl sighed, picked up her bag and together they made their way to the door. 'I don't think they would really approve. Mum will want the big white wedding for me with all the trimmings.'

'Won't you want that?' asked Ali, holding the door open.

'Well, yes, I suppose so.' Jessica shrugged. 'But these days it seems to be the thing to do to try things out first, doesn't it?'

'Yes,' Ali nodded, 'that does seem to be the way of things, but it would have been much different for your parents in their day. They probably wouldn't have dreamt of living together before they were married.'

'So they can't really judge, can they?' said Jessica. 'What about you? What do you think?'

'Me?' Ali threw her a startled glance.

'Yes, would you consider living with someone?'

Ali gave a short laugh. 'I not only considered it. I did it.'

'Did you?' Jessica looked surprised, and Ali wondered how much older than her the girl thought she was.

'Yes, for two years,' she added.

'So did it work? Honestly?' asked Jessica curiously.

'No. It was an absolute disaster,' Ali replied and, seeing Jessica's look of amazement, she added, 'I suppose that isn't entirely fair.'

'There must have been some good times,' protested Jessica as they reached the main entrance. 'If there weren't, why did you stay?'

'Yes.' Ali gave a bleak smile. 'Yes, there were good times—of course there were but. . .' she shrugged '. . .I don't know. . .we were very young and I don't suppose either of us were ready to settle down. There's a certain degree of responsibility to each other even when you are only living together.'

'So what happened?' asked Jessica, obviously still curious.

'The relationship just wasn't going anywhere,' said Ali, 'and if that happens to a relationship,' she added, 'it just fizzles out and dies.'

They paused outside the staff entrance. 'So what

would you do, if you were me?' asked Jessica with a frown.

'What I said,' Ali replied. 'If you don't feel you are ready, then don't.'

Jessica looked down and began kicking at a tuft of grass beside the path with the toe of her boot. 'I'm afraid I might lose him,' she muttered.

'You won't,' said Ali gently. 'Not if he loves you. And if he doesn't, well, he's not worth bothering about.'

'No, I suppose not.' Jessica looked up in surprise. 'Thanks,' she said after a moment, then with a faint smile she turned away and began to walk disconsolately across the grass in the direction of the nurses' home.

Thoughtfully Ali watched her go. There must have been good times, the girl had said. Of course there had been good times. So many good times. But she mustn't think of that now, especially with what was happening. Abruptly she turned away and began to walk to the bicycle shed. There had also been the bad times, and in the end they had outweighed the good.

Thankfully there had been no sign of Connor at the end of the shift and Ali presumed that he must have already left the hospital—either that or he was attending the same meeting as Harvey.

She wheeled her bicycle out of the shed, put her bag in the basket on the handlebars and, mounting, rode down the drive to the main entrance and out onto the road.

It was another balmy May evening, the air thick with the scent of blossom, but as she took the road home between well-tended gardens and neat privet hedges Ali's heart was heavy. She still could hardly believe what had happened. That all this could be about to end. That she would now have to look not only for another job but also for somewhere else to live.

Harvey had told her not to make any decision until

she had slept on the matter, but she didn't have to do that—she knew that even after doing so her decision would be the same. She simply wasn't prepared to put her emotions at risk again from a possible onslaught by Connor Stevens.

She was in no doubt at all that that was what would happen if she was foolish enough to give it the chance. Hadn't it happened before? Not just once but on each occasion when they had parted, on his pleading and persuasion, on her relenting and taking him back—only for the same thing to happen again. . .and again.

No, she thought as she turned the corner of Church Close, there had to be a limit to how much the heart could endure.

So lost had she become in her thoughts that she jumped violently as a car suddenly pulled up alongside her, making her elderly bicycle wobble precariously. The driver of the car wound down the window.

'Hi, there. So is this where you live?'

To her dismay Ali realised that it was Connor.

Her first reaction was to lie. To say she was visiting someone so that he wouldn't know where she lived.

Ignoring him, she dismounted and pushed her bike the last few yards while he parked his car by the kerb, switched off the engine and got out.

'Nice quiet little place,' he said, glancing round at the close. 'Been here long?'

'About eighteen months,' she replied stiffly.

'Flat or house?' He looked up critically at the old, mellow-bricked buildings.

'House, actually.'

'Granny die, did she?'

'I beg your pardon!'

'The old lady? Die and leave it all to you, did she?' He chuckled. 'You always were her favourite, weren't you?'

'I'm sorry, Connor—' she took a deep breath, angered by his audacity even if he had hit on the truth '—but I really don't have the time to stand here talking.' She glanced at her watch. 'I have things to do.'

'You mean you aren't going to ask me in?' He looked genuinely amazed.

'That's the last thing I had in mind.'

'Oh?' He had stopped looking at the house, his gaze instead roaming over her and making her feel decidedly uncomfortable. 'And there was me thinking. . .' He broke off. Ali was never to know what he had been thinking for he suddenly bent down and with a smile said, 'Well, at least someone is pleased to see me. . .'

Boy Blue had run from the garden, his tail in the air, and, ignoring Ali, made a beeline for Connor and was rubbing himself around his legs, a look of pure ecstasy on his face.

Ali watched with mixed feelings as Connor crouched down and fondled the cat, sending it into further raptures of delight.

'You remember me, don't you, old boy?' he murmured then, glancing up at Ali he said, 'How old is he now?'

'Five,' she replied abruptly.

'Of course,' he said softly and, straightening up again but still looking down at Boy Blue, he went on, 'I remember the day you got him. Tiny little thing he was—just a ball of fluff, really. Do you remember the way he used to climb the curtains—those pink ones in the flat—and swing on them?'

'How could I ever forget?' Ali felt her lips twitch into a smile in spite of herself.

'I didn't like those curtains either.' Connor laughed and quick to sense her change of mood, however slight, seized on it and said, 'So do I get to come in now?'

She hesitated. She didn't want him to come in; didn't

want to have to cope with all the painful memories that inevitably would be stirred up. It had started already with his recalling the antics of Boy Blue. She wasn't sure that she could cope with more, but in the end her hesitation was her undoing.

'I promise I'll behave myself,' he said solemnly, but when she glanced sharply at him she saw the blue eyes were brimming with amusement.

'Too right you will,' she replied tightly, wheeling her bicycle down the side of the house and propping it against the wall.

'We do need to talk,' he said as she unlocked the front door and he followed her inside.

'I can't think what about.' Her reply was crisp as she hurried through the hall to the kitchen and dumped her bag on the worktop. 'I must feed Boy Blue,' she said, opening the fridge. 'He'll go frantic if I don't.'

'We need to talk about our jobs,' he said, following her into the kitchen and watching as she opened a tin of cat food and filled Boy Blue's dish. 'I don't intend giving up a position I've only just secured. On the other hand, I see no earthly reason why you should give up your job either just because of what happened between us in the past.'

'I told you, Connor,' she said, placing the spoon she'd used for the cat food in the sink and turning on the tap, 'I prefer not to work with you. If the only way that can happen is for me to go, then I am prepared to do just that.'

'But that's ludicrous,' he protested. 'Good jobs aren't that easy to come by, for God's sake.'

'I know.' Resting her hands on the edge of the sink, she leaned forward slightly and watched the water as it swirled down the drain. Suddenly she was very aware of him behind her, and desperately she wished she wasn't.

'There has to be another way round this. . .'

Vaguely she was aware that he was speaking again, but she would have been unable to say what he had been talking about.

'How did you know I was in Denehurst?' Her hands tightened on the sink and she lowered her head, waiting for his answer.

'What makes you think I did?' he asked lightly at last.

She stiffened, then slowly turned to face him. 'Well, it could hardly have been a coincidence.'

'Couldn't it?' He raised his eyebrows.

She stared at him. 'Denehurst isn't exactly on the beaten track.'

'Maybe not.' He shrugged, turning his head to watch Boy Blue who, having wolfed down his meal, was sitting in the middle of the kitchen floor washing his paws. 'But jobs are still advertised in the medical journals whether they happen to be on the beaten track or not. I saw the job of CO and fancied it. It's as simple as that.'

'So you are saying it was a coincidence?' She stared at him in amazement.

'Did I ever say it wasn't?'

She continued to stare at him, then abruptly turned back to the sink. 'I suppose not,' she muttered. 'I just assumed.'

'You assumed I had tracked you down,' he said softly, 'didn't you, Ali?'

'You tried to once before,' she retorted quickly, accusingly.

'Did I?' Again the eyebrows were raised. 'Well, maybe I did.' He gave a slight shrug. 'But that was a long time ago, Ali. A lot of water has flowed under the bridge since then. You have obviously built a life for yourself—' he glanced round as he spoke '—and so have I.' He paused and then suddenly took a step towards her.

'Listen,' he said and as she flattened herself against the worktop he held up his hands in a rueful gesture, 'listen, Ali, please. I haven't come here to make trouble for you—you have to believe that. I was pleased to see you—I don't deny that. What we had once was very special but, like I say, that's all in the past now. We are probably two different people now—we simply can't let what happened then jeopardise what is happening now.'

Suddenly she wished that she could accept what he was saying. Wanted to accept it, in fact, but still she couldn't quite get over the feeling that he had in some way contrived the whole thing. If, on the other hand, it was as he was saying and he had come to Denehurst and St Mark's quite by chance, maybe she should just accept the situation. She raised her eyes and let her gaze meet his. But could she trust herself? Trust herself to be with him, work with him, be close to him every day?

'How have you left things with Harvey?' he asked after a moment.

'He told me to sleep on it before deciding,' she replied.

'Very wise. He doesn't want to lose you, Ali. He told me what a valuable member of the team you are and how much he has come to rely on you.'

'Harvey said that?' She raised a sceptical eyebrow and Connor had the grace to grin.

'Well, maybe not in those exact words,' he admitted, 'but the sentiments were the same. Come on, Ali—' there was a pleading note in his voice now '—say you'll stay; say you'll give it a try.'

Still she hesitated. Still there was a niggle at the back of her mind that somehow he would manipulate her into going back to him.

'Ali?' He reached out his hand and would have

touched her arm but instinctively she drew back, and in that second the doorbell rang.

With a sigh Connor lowered his hand and Ali hurried to answer the door.

Maggie stood on the doorstep. 'Hello,' she said, 'I was worried about you. Thought I'd pop round.'

Ali gave a wan smile. 'You'd better come in,' she said. She didn't know whether she was pleased or disappointed to see her friend at that precise moment. Turning, she led the way through the hall to the kitchen.

'I missed you at the end of the shift,' Maggie said as she followed her. 'Did you get to speak to Harvey—Oh!' she broke off sharply as she entered the kitchen and caught sight of Connor lounging against the worktop. 'Oh, I'm sorry,' she said, glancing at Ali, clearly embarrassed at finding him there, 'I didn't know you had anyone here.'

'Don't mind me,' said Connor.

'No, don't mind him,' echoed Ali quickly. 'Besides, he was just leaving.'

'Was I?' Connor raised his eyebrows then, catching sight of Ali's expression, he unfolded his arms and eased himself away from the worktop.

'Connor was just passing,' she said, not wanting Maggie to get the wrong impression, and glancing at him, she added, 'I presume you were on your way home?'

He inclined his head slightly. 'Yes,' he agreed, 'yes, you could say that.' The blue eyes were full of amusement again.

'So where is home?' asked Maggie, apparently fully recovered from the shock of finding him there.

'Greyfriars—it's an old monastery converted into apartments.'

'I know it well,' replied Maggie smoothly. 'My brother rented a place there a couple of years ago while he was waiting to go abroad. Very nice.'

'Yes, well, it suits me,' Connor replied, 'and it's reasonably close to the hospital.'

Silence followed his remark. Connor glanced from Ali to Maggie and then back to Ali again. 'Ah, well,' he said at last, 'I guess I'd best be going. See you girls at work tomorrow.' With a nod he strolled out of the kitchen.

Ali threw Maggie a quick grimace before following him to the front door.

'Go and see Harvey tomorrow,' he said, pausing as he opened the door, one hand on the catch, 'and tell him what he wants to hear.'

'Surely that depends on what conclusion I come to after sleeping on the problem?' said Ali coolly.

'Of course,' he replied, equally coolly. 'I'd just hate to see you cut off your nose to spite your face.'

'There's no fear of that,' she replied briskly, at the same time wishing that he would just go.

'Really?' He looked down at her as she continued to stand in the doorway so that, in fact, as she prepared to close the door behind him they were standing very close to each other.

For a moment their eyes met and it seemed in that instant that the whole of the two years they had spent together was there in that look. Every conversation they had ever had. Every experience they had shared.

Gradually, even as she watched, she saw his eyes darken and his expression change from one of quizzical amusement to one that she found impossible to define.

Then, with a muttered exclamation, he was gone, moving rapidly away down the path.

She closed the door behind him and found that she was shaking. For one moment, in an effort to recover before she went back to Maggie, she leaned against the door.

Why, oh, why had she let him in? She had known that it would be a mistake.

From outside she heard the sound of his car as he started the engine and as the car drew away and the sound eventually faded into the distance she looked up and found Maggie standing in the kitchen doorway watching her.

'Shall I put the kettle on?' she said.

'I think I need something a bit stronger than tea,' Ali replied, walking slowly back down the hall. 'There's a bottle of wine in the fridge,' she added as she reached the kitchen.

'Now you're talking.' Maggie opened the fridge door and Ali took two glasses from the cupboard.

'So he was just passing?' Maggie watched as she poured the wine.

'Apparently.'

'He was obviously taking the scenic route home.' Maggie observed drily.

'What do you mean?' Ali frowned as she passed her a glass.

'Greyfriars is out on the Winchester road on the far side of Denehurst.'

'Is that a fact?' Ali looked up. 'Well, I suppose that doesn't really surprise me.' She paused. 'What I do find unbelievable is the idea of Connor Stevens living in a monastery!' She gave a short laugh. 'Shall we take this and sit outside?'

'Why not? This warm weather can't last much longer.' Sipping her wine, Maggie followed her into the sitting-room and watched as she unlocked the French doors.

'So what did he want?' she asked.

'To talk, or so he said. He'd obviously spoken to Harvey.'

'Who'd no doubt told him of your intentions to look

for another job.' Maggie followed her outside and they both sat down, Ali on the wooden bench seat and Maggie on one of two white wrought-iron garden chairs. 'So what was his reaction?'

Ali shrugged. 'He seems to think there's no need for me to go. That there's room for both of us at St Mark's.'

'And what about you?' Maggie set her glass down on a table that matched the white chairs. 'What do you think?'

'He's probably right. I dare say there is room for both of us. . .' Ali trailed off and lifted her face to the last of the day's sun, closing her eyes and luxuriating in its warmth.

'I detect a ''but'' coming,' said Maggie drily.

'Do you now?' Ali opened one eye and when Maggie nodded she sighed. 'You're absolutely right. We could work together, but that doesn't mean to say I want to work with him.'

'Could one be forgiven for asking why?'

Ali sighed, an impatient sigh. 'I've been down that road before,' she said sharply.

'It might be different this time.'

'True, but I'm not even sure I want to find out.'

They lapsed into silence. Around them was the still of the fragrant summer evening and the gently lengthening shadows, the only sounds those of a distant lawnmower and the faint hum of the traffic on the nearby dual carriageway.

'Do you know,' said Ali at last, breaking the silence between them and picking up her glass again, 'do you know, he would even have me believe his coming to Denehurst, to St Mark's, was a coincidence. . .?'

They were silent again and this time it was Maggie who eventually spoke. 'Do you think,' she said, throwing Ali a quick, uncertain glance, 'do you think it simply might have been that?'

'No chance!' snapped Ali.

'No, of course not,' Maggie agreed.

They sat on, enjoying the last of the sunshine. Ali topped up their glasses.

'So you think,' said Maggie reflectively, at last, 'that he somehow tracked you down here?'

'It wouldn't be the first time he's tried to find me.'

'Presumably he failed before.'

'Yes. . .'

'Right, so this time he succeeds,' said Maggie thoughtfully. 'He finds you; he even gets a job in the same hospital and finds accommodation—some lengths, really, especially for someone you said wasn't interested in long-term commitment. . .'

'He wasn't,' said Ali sharply.

'But could that not simply have been because of his age. . .immaturity. . .?'

'No,' said Ali, 'there was more to it than that. I found out during the time we were together that his parents had split up when he was a boy. It was particularly traumatic and I think it put him off marriage—I can't see he's changed his attitude since.'

'OK,' Maggie shrugged. 'So, what are his motives, do you think?'

'I know exactly what his motives are,' said Ali tersely. 'He wants to carry on where we left off.'

'What—three years ago? That's a long time, Ali.'

'Maybe.' She shook her head almost angrily. 'But I know him, Maggie; he wants to have his cake and eat it too.'

'Right.' Maggie spread her hands in a gesture of acquiescence. 'I accept what you're saying. So, he wants you back. Is that so terrible?'

'I couldn't,' cried Ali passionately. 'I just couldn't. You don't know what you're asking. I simply couldn't go through it all again. It's taken me years to get over him.'

'All right, Ali. All right, don't get upset. I understand. I really do. I have been through a divorce, don't forget.'

Ali looked up sharply. 'Sorry,' she mumbled. For the moment she had forgotten.

They fell silent yet again, each reflecting, then Maggie said, 'Treat you badly, did he?'

'Well. . .'

'Knock you about?'

'Of course not!' Ali looked up sharply, her eyes meeting Maggie's. 'Did Ted. . .?'

'No.' Maggie shook her head. 'No. . . In fact, I hit him.'

'You. . .?' Ali stared at her friend incredulously.

'Yes. I nearly killed him.'

'But why? I wouldn't have put you down as a violent type.'

'I'm not. . .usually,' said Maggie. 'I found out he was having an affair with a friend of mine. After I'd nearly killed him, I filed for divorce.'

'Oh, dear, I'm sorry.' Ali sighed. 'I didn't know. Oh, I knew you were divorced, of course,' she added hurriedly, 'but I didn't know the circumstances. So what happened. . .to Ted, I mean. . .? Did he. . .did he. . .?'

'Marry my friend?' Maggie raised her eyebrows. 'No, of course he didn't. They rarely do, you know. He married someone else. Now that marriage has broken up. I saw him recently. . .and he looked so. . . defeated. . . Do you know, Ali, I could have wept. He nearly destroyed me at the time and I hated him; wouldn't take him back when he begged me to; thought I could never trust him again, but now I wonder what it was all about. . .' She shrugged and Ali saw the gleam of tears in her eyes.

'Are you saying you should have taken him back?

Should have given him another chance?' Ali stared at her in astonishment.

'I don't know, Ali. I really don't. All I do know is we were so happy once and then came all the misery. Now, well, Ted isn't happy. . .'

'But you are, aren't you?'

'I don't know,' said Maggie. 'I think it was all such a waste. And I think that in your case, Ali, what I am trying to say is don't be too hasty. Don't do something that you could live to regret.'

It was all very well for Maggie to say that, Ali thought later, long after her friend had gone and she was preparing for bed. She didn't know the full story—people never did when they told you what you should or shouldn't do. They only based their theories on their own experiences, which were always far different from your own.

She didn't want to leave her job—of course she didn't; neither did she want to lose her home nor the new friends she had made. But could she trust herself working with Connor; could she trust herself not to fall in love with him again?

The other question she had to face was whether she had, in fact, actually stopped loving him or whether she had been deluding herself.

Sleep eluded her for a long time and she found herself going over and over in her mind the time when she and Connor had finally parted. It had been something really quite trivial that had sparked the row, as those things usually are. They had both been invited to a colleague's wedding and Connor had failed to turn up—in fact, he hadn't even returned to the flat, following the groom's stag night.

For Ali it had been the final straw—the last in a long line of similar incidents—and she had finally, from somewhere, found the courage to end the relationship.

She knew from past experience that Connor would try to come back, just as she knew that in a moment of weakness she would take him back, so this time she had left her job at the hospital where they both worked, had given up her flat and returned for a time to her parents' home.

From there she had moved to another hospital, this time in the north-east, and then eventually south, to Denehurst and St Mark's, in the hopes of building a new life for herself.

And she had been winning. She was sure she'd been winning. Until now. Until Connor Stevens had strolled back into her life and once again created problems that she did not know how to solve. When eventually she fell asleep it was in the hopes that somehow, overnight, she would miraculously find an answer to these problems and know what she had to do.

CHAPTER FIVE

SHE dreamt about him again that night, vivid dreams in which he pursued her relentlessly. They were on a beach at night; moonlight was sparkling on the sea and the sand was wet and hard. When he finally caught her they ended up making love at the water's edge with the surf breaking over them. It was every bit as wonderful as it had always been and so real, so very, very real.

She awoke shaking, her heart pounding. It was barely dawn and she lay for a long time staring at the ceiling and watching as the room slowly grew lighter. Outside the window the birds were in full chorus, but when at last she ventured to turn her head and look at her bedside clock she found that it was only five o'clock. With a groan she turned over. She knew she wouldn't be able to go back to sleep again. But at least she now knew what she had to do.

She would go and see Harvey as soon as she got to work.

Ali always enjoyed her ride to work. Somehow it seemed to set her up for the day and whatever might be waiting for her. But that morning she heard the klaxons when she was still a fair distance from the hospital and when three ambulances overtook her she knew that they had a full-scale emergency on their hands.

Hurrying onto the unit, she found the place swarming with paramedics and police. The night staff were still on duty and Ali saw Elizabeth Malchin, the senior night sister, in the nurses' station briefing Harvey, who had also just arrived and who hadn't even had a chance to change into his uniform.

'What is it, Di?' Ali leaned across the reception desk.

'A train crash.' The receptionist was wide-eyed. 'Someone said the six forty-five hit another train.'

'How many casualties?'

'Not sure exactly. We've been told to prepare for a lot. Winchester is also standing by.'

Ali ran to the nurses' room, tearing off her clothes as she went and then quite literally throwing on her uniform. She was still fastening her belt as she ran back down the corridor to the nurses' station. Harvey, who by this time was wearing his white coat, turned sharply from the blackboard.

'Treatment room, please, Ali,' was all he said, but it was enough. She nodded and even as she hurried forward two more paramedics arrived with another patient on a trolley.

As the doors of both treatment rooms swung back and forth Ali caught glimpses of frenzied activity. The moment she entered one of the rooms she was pounced upon by the night sister who, together with the rest of her shift, had volunteered to remain on duty.

In the midst of the pandemonium her brain registered that Connor was in the room and, together with Samara, seemed to be fighting to resuscitate a young man with appalling head injuries. Then the moment was gone, and immediately she was drawn into the business of saving lives.

Gradually as she worked, identifying patients, assessing injuries, evaluating, carrying out emergency procedures and reassuring those who were able to understand, Ali picked up further details of what had happened. The train, an early-morning commuter train bound for London, had careered into the back of a goods train. Some passengers had been crushed on impact and others had been shunted forward while some, including the driver, were still being cut from the wreckage.

Inevitably, with an incident of such proportions, there were fatalities—some at the scene, others dying in ambulances *en route* to hospital and still others while they were being assessed.

A major incident plan had been put into operation at St Mark's, with extra beds and blankets immediately being made available in the casualty department. A notice posted at the entrance informed the public that delays would be inevitable and only extreme emergencies would be dealt with.

The accident and emergency team under their casualty consultant, Francis Braithwaite, were pushed to the limits of their resources and eventually more staff were called in from other departments to assist. Relief theatre, X-ray and pathology staff were put on standby, while the wards, as each patient was categorised, prepared for a sudden influx. The blood bank was contacted and preparations were made to transfer huge quantities of blood supplies to Denehurst.

'Relatives are beginning to arrive,' said Harvey as he escorted yet another patient into the treatment room, 'but at the moment I can't spare anyone to talk to them.'

'Many of the patients are young people,' said Connor, turning from one of the beds.

'That means we shall have distraught parents to cope with soon,' observed Harvey. 'I'll get on to Welfare to give us a hand.'

'They must be secretaries and office staff who were going into work in the City,' said Ali sadly, looking down at a young woman on the bed who had failed to respond to all their attempts at resuscitation. Her blonde hair was spread out on the pillow and around her neck she still wore a gold pendant inscribed with the name 'Susan'. Something about her reminded Ali of Jessica.

'Where's Jessica Lake this morning?' she called after Harvey as he reached the doors.

'I put her on walking wounded,' he said. 'I thought it best.'

Ali nodded, and with a sigh pushed the hair from her eyes.

'You OK?'

She looked up sharply and found Connor watching her. 'Of course. Why shouldn't I be?'

'No reason—I just wondered. You used to get pretty upset at this sort of thing, if I remember rightly.'

'I was a student in those days,' she retorted.

'And now you're a fully-fledged senior staff nurse,' he said softly.

'It makes a difference—' She broke off, not certain that he wasn't mocking her.

He had discarded his white coat and his tie, and was working with the top few buttons of his shirt undone and his sleeves rolled up. His dark hair was as untidy as ever, his eyes heavy-lidded and sexily attractive. The overall impression was so reminiscent of the old Connor that as Ali suddenly remembered her dream of the night before she felt the blood rush to her face.

Their lovemaking in the dream had been just like it used to be—she could still feel the weight of his body, the feel of his skin against hers and the taste of his kisses mingled with the salt water of the sea. . .

Abruptly, almost angrily, she checked herself. What in the world was she thinking of, allowing such thoughts to fill her mind, and at such a time as well? She straightened up, automatically smoothing down the plastic apron she wore to protect her uniform.

'Penny for them?'

When she looked up sharply it was to find Connor still watching her closely. 'What do you mean?' she almost snapped, so immersed had she become in her thoughts.

'Your thoughts. You were miles away.' The expression in his eyes and the smile that lurked around the corners of his lips suggested that he knew exactly what she had been thinking.

But that was ridiculous. How could he know? Her thoughts had not even been of reality—had centred purely on a dream.

The fact that he had shared the dream was neither here nor there.

'I was merely concentrating on the job in hand,' she replied primly, but even as she said it she knew that he didn't believe her. He knew her too well. Damn him. She turned away. Why had he come back? She had got used to him not being around; had been getting her life back together again. . . Now. . .

Her frustration was brought to an abrupt end by the arrival of yet another patient, this time a middle-aged man in his pin-striped city suit.

Immediately they were caught up in the relentless round of assessment and evaluation again.

The rest of the morning seemed to merge into a blur: the setting up of one infusion after another; the cutting of clothing from badly injured limbs; the administration of pain-killing injections; fitting of catheters and positioning of splints. And for the more experienced staff like Ali came the job of assisting the doctors with more complex procedures, such as inserting chest drains to relieve collapsed lungs, or cardiac massage or defibrillation if a patient suddenly arrested.

And throughout it all ran the medical staff's reassurances—talking to patients who could hear, explaining to them what was happening, promising to find out what had happened to companions or loved ones, and calming and emphasising that everything was going to be all right.

'Really,' said Maggie, in a lull between crises, 'we go into automatic pilot when something like this happens.'

'The adrenalin takes over,' observed Francis Braithwaite, peering at them all owl-like through his horn-rimmed glasses before turning to Maggie and saying, 'Could you get the orthopaedic registrar on the phone again, please? I can't imagine they've got any beds left up there, but we can hardly put a patient with two fractured femurs anywhere else.'

The lull was short-lived as another wave of patients arrived, this time those who had been trapped and cut free by the rescue services.

Around lunchtime, as the situation began to ease a little, Harvey started to organise staff breaks.

On her way to the staff-room Ali was waylaid in Reception by a very irate man, who proceeded to inform her that he had been waiting for hours and demanded to know if she had any idea when he could expect to be seen.

'Did you check in at Reception when you arrived?' she asked.

'Of course I did,' he snapped, 'but that was hours ago. All these people keep coming in and are being seen before me.'

'We do have a major incident on our hands—' Ali struggled to stay calm '—and most of those people were very badly injured.'

'How do you know that I'm not very badly injured?' the man demanded, his eyes glittering.

'So tell me, what is your problem Mr. . .?'

'The name's Leithwood,' the man replied, 'and I think I may have sprained my wrist.'

'Did you not read the notice outside?' asked Ali. 'We

are only dealing with the most urgent emergencies at the moment.'

'So what am I supposed to do?' The man began to go red in the face. 'You just tell me that.'

'Well, you could go to your GP, to a pharmacist for advice or to another casualty unit,' Ali began patiently, but the man interrupted her.

'Listen. I have rights, you know, and I know my rights.'

'Of course you do, Mr Leithwood. . .'

'I have just as many rights as these other people. . . You have to watch these things, you know.' He turned away, apparently addressing his remarks to anyone who happened to be listening, then turning back to Ali again and this time pointing his finger at her, he went on, 'You can't turn me away. . .you could be in trouble for that sort of thing, my girl.'

'I was about to say that if you didn't want to go elsewhere you could continue to wait here and you will be seen just as soon as someone is available.'

'And when will that be? That's what I want to know. Nine o'clock it was when I arrived, and look at the time now. . . It's preposterous, that's what it is! And I'm not the only one; there're others here who've been waiting for hours as well—' He turned again, pointing wildly to the waiting area behind him. Ali turned also and saw perhaps half a dozen other patients who had elected to wait to be seen. Most looked resigned to waiting for a long time, a couple looked sheepish at their fellow patient's behaviour, while one woman appeared to have fallen asleep in the corner.

Ali took a deep breath. 'All I can do is apologise,' she said. 'We are doing our best, and if you choose to wait you will be seen eventually.'

The people nodded and shuffled their feet while Mr Leithwood gave a loud snort and stamped back to his

seat, muttering that he would be sending a letter to
his MP.

Moments later Ali found herself in the staff-room
with Beth, Peggy and Connor. They collapsed into easy
chairs while Peggy made them fresh coffee.

'Do we know if all the casualties have been brought
in?' asked Beth, taking a packet of cigarettes from
her bag.

'The last I heard they were still searching the wreckage,' Connor replied, shaking his head as Beth offered
him a cigarette. 'No, thanks,' he said, 'I don't.' Catching
sight of Ali's expression,' he grinned and added, 'I gave
it up, along with a few other things.'

'I wish I could give it up.' Beth lit her cigarette and
inhaled deeply. 'I keep trying, but I don't seem to have
the will-power. The pressures of the job don't help
either.'

'Ah, you need an incentive,' replied Connor.

Ali found herself waiting to see if he would say what
his incentive had been, but he didn't, and somehow she
didn't feel it would be appropriate for her to ask.
Instead, she stood up and walked across to help Peggy
distribute the mugs of steaming coffee.

'That smells good.' Connor looked up at her as she
handed him his mug.

'So the caffeine habit wasn't in the list of vices you
gave up?' she said, raising one eyebrow and trying to
stop her lips from twitching. She knew that she
shouldn't have said it as soon as the words left her lips;
knew that he would read more into it—see it in some
way as a softening of her attitude towards him.

'A man has to be left with something,' he said softly,
looking up at her. As he took the mug his fingers
deliberately touched hers.

She withdrew her hand sharply. To anyone watching
it would have appeared that the heat from the coffee had

burnt her fingers, but she and Connor knew otherwise. Swiftly she moved away from him and sat down again.

They didn't dare take long over their break and barely ten minutes later they made their way back to Reception. When they reached the swing doors Connor held them open and Beth and Peggy walked ahead, leaving Connor holding the door for Ali.

As she passed him in the confined space her shoulder brushed his chest.

'Just like old times, isn't it?' he murmured, so softly that only she heard.

She stopped and as he let the door swing closed she answered over her shoulder, again quietly so that only he heard, 'No, Connor. It isn't like old times at all,' she said, 'and it won't be, not now or ever again, because I won't be around to give it the chance.'

Reception was still in chaos, packed now with friends and relatives of the victims of the train crash, all demanding information and updates. The local vicar of Denehurst was at the desk, talking to Chrissie and two uniformed policemen. A woman sitting in the front row of the chairs appeared to be having hysterics. Someone was sobbing and a young man dressed in jeans and a string vest was demanding loudly that his baby, whom he was carrying in a multicoloured portable car seat, be seen immediately.

Ali walked briskly into the nurses' station. 'Where do you want me, Harvey?' she asked.

The charge nurse looked up wearily. 'I'd like you to give a hand out here, Ali. Oh, Connor,' he added as he caught sight of the CO, 'Mr Braithwaite was looking for you—he's in the treatment room.'

Ali took a deep breath and, as Connor went off down the passage to the treatment rooms, Harvey threw her a quick glance. 'Everything all right, Ali?' he said.

'Yes, fine, Harvey,' she replied firmly, 'just fine. I'll

speak to you later. . .' She trailed off as there came a
sudden commotion in Reception—shouting and the
sound of running feet. She and Harvey glanced at each
other and moved forward to investigate.

'A lady has collapsed,' called Chrissie. 'She's been
sitting over there in the corner. . .I thought she was
asleep. . .'

Joe Freeman, one of the department's porters, ran to
join Harvey and Ali and between them they carried the
woman into a cubicle. Samara was called to examine
her, and she was found to be having a heart attack.

'I feel dreadful,' said Chrissie later after the woman
had been treated and Ali stepped out of the cubicle.
'When she came in she simply said she wasn't feeling
well. I said she might have a long wait because of the
crash and she just went and sat quietly in the corner.
She never complained or anything. . . Not like that Mr
Leithwood—he never stopped complaining and he
started others off as well.'

'Has he been seen now?' asked Ali.

'Yes, Samara saw him. He's gone home.'

'It's so often the ones who make the least fuss who
have the most wrong with them,' said Ali. She looked
round Reception which, if anything, looked more con-
gested than ever then, raising her voice above the
unbelievable level of noise, she said, 'Right, Chrissie,
Harvey wants me to start talking to some of these people
now that it's a bit quieter in the treatment rooms. Where
would you like me to start?'

Chrissie looked round, glanced down at her check-
ing-in record and then back towards the throng of
people. 'I think,' she said, 'that couple over there talking
to Fr. Regan. A Mr and Mrs Phillips. Their daughter
Susan was on the train. . .'

'Right.' Taking a deep breath, Ali moved across
to the anxious-looking couple who were in deep

conversation with the local Catholic priest. 'Mr and Mrs
Phillips?' she asked.

'Yes,' the man nodded.

'Do you have any news for us?' asked Mrs Phillips
eagerly. 'Our daughter, Susan, was brought in here. She
was on her way to work, you know. . .'

'Perhaps you'd like to come into the office,' Ali said
gently. As the couple stood up and moved forward,
Ali caught Fr. Regan's eye and, without a word, he
joined them.

One of the hardest parts of a major incident was dealing
with relatives, and by the time the last of them had left
the accident and emergency unit, either to go to the
wards to visit an injured loved one or to the mortuary
to identify one, the staff were exhausted. By this time
Reception was comparatively clear and the staff congre-
gated around the nurses' station.

'Well done, everyone,' said Harvey. 'It's been quite
a day. One none of us shall forget in a hurry.'

'You can say that again,' said Maggie.

'Do we know any details?' Connor perched on the
edge of the desk.

Harvey glanced down at a report sheet. 'Rumour has
it that signal failure was responsible, but we won't know
that for sure until after the official inquiry. There were
eleven fatalities—four at the scene. Fifty-two people
were injured—twenty-three sustained serious injury.
The majority of those were treated here and the rest
were taken to Winchester.'

'So, all in all, we coped pretty well,' observed Beth.

'No less than I would have expected,' replied Harvey.
'We've got a good team here—' he glanced round
'—when they put their minds to it.' He grinned and
then, as if suddenly remembering something, he looked
at Connor. 'Talking of teams, in all the excitement I

haven't really had the chance to welcome Dr Stevens aboard.'

Connor laughed. 'You just organised a baptism of fire instead. Do you try out all your new CO's like this?'

Ali found herself joining in the general laughter but rapidly grew serious again. Just for one moment she'd forgotten that soon she would no longer be part of that team. She winced as the reality hit her.

Was there a possibility that she had overreacted? Could she not stay and work alongside him?

Raising her head, she looked across at him sitting so casually on the edge of the desk.

As if he sensed her scrutiny and the soul-searching that accompanied it he glanced up, caught her eye and winked—the gesture both familiar and conspiratorial. In doing so he gave Ali her answer.

She couldn't put her newly won peace of mind at risk again, leaving her emotions open to another onslaught from this man.

'Thanks for your welcome.' She realised that Connor was speaking again. 'I'm happy to be aboard and, in all seriousness, if today was an example of the teamwork in this unit then I'm happy to be part of it.'

'What made you choose St Mark's?' someone called across the station.

Connor looked up and Ali suddenly found herself holding her breath as she waited for his reply.

He seemed to hesitate. To anyone who didn't know him the pause was imperceptible but to Ali, who knew him so well, it was obvious that he was choosing his words with care. 'It offered,' he said at last, 'the post I wanted, career-wise—'

'It's hardly the hub of modern technology,' someone else observed caustically.

'Maybe not,' Connor gave his easy, almost lazy laugh, 'but there was other method in my madness. . .'

'Now we're getting to it. . .!'

Ali realised that her hands were clenched into tight fists.

'It enables me to be near a certain lady,' said Connor smoothly.

Ali glanced sharply at him but he was staring at the floor.

'There has to be a woman in it,' said Joe Freeman with a laugh. 'There's always a woman behind these things.'

'So, who is she, Connor?' said Beth. 'Anyone we know?'

'It's the lady I hope to marry,' said Connor quietly. 'And, no, I doubt whether any of you know her.' He glanced round at the circle of faces as he spoke. 'She lives in Winchester,' he added, 'but she's only just moved to the area.'

The phone rang at that moment. Harvey answered it and Di appeared with a message for Samara from Mr Braithwaite.

For Ali it took that long for what Connor had just said to sink in. She was vaguely aware of Maggie's concerned stare; of the fact that Connor had turned away and was laughing at something that Joe had just said, and then of her own overwhelming need to get out of the nurses' station—out of the building which had become suddenly claustrophobic—to seek some fresh air to counteract the shock she had received.

And it had been a shock; there was no denying that.

God, what a fool she'd been. What an utter fool. Imagining he'd come to Denehurst because he'd tracked her down. Thinking he'd taken the job at St Mark's to be near her in order to resume their relationship. . .when all the time. . .all the time. . .he had another woman.

A woman who lived in Winchester; a woman who had only recently moved into the area. And this woman,

whoever she was, was the woman he'd said he hoped
to marry.

Oh God, who had she told?

Maggie. . .and Harvey. . . That was all. Had she actually told Harvey? She couldn't remember. But she knew
she'd told Maggie. Whatever must she think of her?
How could she have been so egotistical? And Connor
himself! What in the world had she said to him? She'd
made it plain she didn't want to work with him, but
had she said why? Had she made it obvious that she'd
thought he'd wanted her back?

Later she couldn't remember changing out of her
uniform into her outdoor clothes because at the time
she'd been in a daze. The first thing she really became
aware of was Maggie, hurrying outside to join her.

'Are you OK, Ali?'

'Yes, fine. Fine,' she repeated then, putting her head
down, she hurried off in the direction of the
bicycle shed.

'Hang on a minute!' Maggie ran after her and grabbed
her arm. 'Don't go rushing off. You're upset.'

'No, no, I'm not. I'm fine. Absolutely fine,' she
gulped, stopping as Maggie turned her around to
face her.

'Rubbish!' snapped Maggie. 'You've had a shock.
Listen, are you in a hurry?'

She shook her head. Suddenly her voice seemed to
have deserted her.

'Good. I've got my car. Leave your bike here. We'll
nip down into Denehurst—to that little teashop. I'll
bring you back here afterwards to get your bike.'

Ali didn't want to go to the teashop. She wanted to
go home to get away from everyone—to come to terms
with her humiliation in private—but then, out of the
corner of her eye, she caught a glimpse of Connor
coming out of the accident and emergency entrance. He

was talking to Beth and Mac, but he saw her. She knew he'd seen her. In a moment he would leave the others and come across to her.

She panicked. 'All right, Maggie,' she said, 'let's go.'

CHAPTER SIX

'I FEEL such a fool.' Ali stared miserably at the crisp, white tablecloth.

'I don't see why.' Maggie poured tea into delicate china cups. 'How could you have known that it was merely a coincidence, after all?'

'It just seemed so improbable, that's all. I mean, Denehurst of all places.'

'Yes, and the fact that he had tried to find you before—don't forget that, Ali. It's no wonder you jumped to the wrong conclusion. Here, have a piece of ginger cake—it's very good.'

'I'm really not hungry. . .'

'Go on.'

'Oh, all right. . .' With a sigh Ali took a small piece of ginger cake. Suddenly she was glad she'd come with Maggie, in spite of the fact that in the first place she'd wanted to go straight home.

The Olde Worlde Tea Shoppe in the High Street at Denehurst was almost deserted that afternoon, which wasn't really surprising when one considered that the small population of the town would be reeling from the aftermath of the train disaster on its doorstep and in no mood to sit in teashops. The windows were open and a light breeze drifted through the beamed, low-ceilinged rooms, carrying with it the scent of lavender and herbs from the garden at the rear.

Gradually Ali felt herself relax and it was only then that she realised just how uptight she had become over the whole situation.

'At least it's solved the main problem,' remarked

Maggie, as she popped a piece of ginger cake into her mouth.

'What has?' Ali stared at her friend over the rim of her cup.

'Him having another woman.'

'What do you mean?' Ali frowned.

'Well, you won't have to think about getting another job now, will you?'

'I. . , Well, I don't know, Maggie.' She set her cup back into its saucer. 'I'm still not sure I particularly want to work with him.'

'You said before you didn't want to work with him because you didn't want him trying to start up your relationship again.'

'I know, but. . .'

'He's hardly going to do that if he's thinking of marrying someone else, is he?'

'No, I suppose not. . .' she said slowly.

'And you don't want him thinking it bothers you that he has someone else, do you?'

'No. . .'

'Well, that's what he will think if you still refuse to work with him.' Maggie raised one eyebrow. 'Come on, Ali, think about it,' she added. 'You don't want him assuming that, do you?'

'Of course I don't.' Her reply was emphatic. That was the last thing she wanted. She shuddered at the thought.

'Unless, of course,' Maggie went on a moment later, lifting the lid of the teapot and peering inside, 'unless. . .'

'Unless what?' Ali demanded.

'Unless it really does bother you.' Maggie replaced the lid. 'More tea?'

Ali nodded absent-mindedly. 'Of course it doesn't bother me,' she said as she watched Maggie pour second

cups of tea and add milk. 'I told you before that whatever there was between me and Connor Stevens was
well and truly over—a very long time ago.'

'In that case,' replied Maggie firmly, adding a spoon-
ful of sugar to her tea, 'nothing need change and we
can all get on with our work. . .just like we did before
he came on the scene. . .' Having stirred her tea, she
replaced the spoon in the saucer with a flourish, took
a sip and sat back in her chair. Then, as if the thought
had only just occurred to her, she said, 'I say, you
hadn't given Harvey your notice, had you?'

'No.' Ali, watching her, shook her head. 'No, I
hadn't.'

'Well, thank goodness for that.' Maggie gave a sigh
of relief. 'I shouldn't say any more to Harvey if I were
you, unless he asks, of course—just carry on as if
nothing had happened.'

If only it were that easy, thought Ali. If only she
could simply pretend that nothing had happened. But it
had happened, whether she liked to admit it or not. She
was grateful to Maggie for her kind concern but she
was relieved when she finally got home and she and
Boy Blue shut the front door on the rest of the world.

It had been a shock to discover that Connor was
going to marry someone else, almost as much of a shock
as it had been to have him stroll back into her life. She
wasn't sure yet which was worse—the thought that he
might have wanted her back or the thought of him
with someone else. The idea of working with him and
knowing that he was wanting to revive their relationship
had been more than she could cope with, but the idea
of working with him and knowing he was so heavily
involved with someone else? How would she cope with
that? She quite simply didn't know.

But Maggie was right—she had to do it if she didn't
want Connor to think she was bothered by the fact that

he had another woman. And the very thought of him thinking that made her squirm.

No, she told herself firmly as she prowled restlessly round the house that evening, she wouldn't give him that satisfaction. She would calmly carry on with her job, treating him no differently than she would any other member of staff.

But later, much later, as she lay and relaxed in her bath she found her thoughts wandering again.

What was she like, this other woman? All Connor had said was that she had recently come to live in Winchester. That didn't really tell her very much. Was she younger than her, or older? Was she tall or short? Fat or thin? Dark or fair?

The only thing Connor had said was that he had taken the job in Denehurst—a virtual backwater—just to be near her.

He must love her very much.

Ali slipped further down in the bath, immersing her shoulders in the soft bubbles.

Of course he loved her. He had said that he hoped to marry her. No one would say that they hoped to marry someone unless they really loved them, for heaven's sake.

Vigorously she soaped her arms. The other way round could be so, of course. Someone could tell you that they loved you, but not want to marry you.

He had told her that he loved her. Many times. But he'd never asked her to marry him. Almost ferociously she ducked her head right under the water.

What if he had? She surfaced, the water pouring from her hair and running in rivulets down her face, neck and shoulders. Would it have made any difference? Would she have agreed? Stayed with him?

How could she know the answer to that? The question was purely hypothetical. He had not asked her to marry him; had quite obviously not loved her enough for that, while she—at the end of her tether with his wild, erratic ways—had left him.

This other woman, whoever she was, obviously was able to cope with his behaviour. Or maybe Connor himself had changed. Maybe he'd grown up. Matured. Learned to love someone enough to marry them. . . Her breath caught suddenly in her throat.

Was it as good with this woman when he made love to her as it had been between them? Because it had been good. Hadn't it? That hadn't been a figment of her imagination—a trick of memory?

She knew it hadn't. Why, if she closed her eyes and concentrated, she could still, after all this time, slip her mind back and remember in minute detail how it had been.

How he would whisper her name whilst arousing her, his fingers sliding across her skin, his tongue softly teasing until her body ached for him. How their loving would last far into the night as they brought each other time and again to the very brink of ecstasy until the moment when at last they would soar together. And how afterwards, utterly fulfilled in each other's arms, they would sleep. . .

The sound of the telephone broke into her thoughts, fragmenting her memories with its persistent intrusion.

With a sigh she sat up, realising that the water had grown cold. Stepping from the bath, she wrapped herself in a towel, padded through to the bedroom and lifted the receiver of her bedside phone.

Because she had been so embroiled in memories of Connor, she thought for one wild moment that it would be his voice that she would hear.

'Hello, Ali. It's Harvey.'

'Oh, Harvey.' She was almost disappointed.

'Have I caught you at a bad moment?'

'Not unless you call getting out of the bath a bad moment.'

'I'm sorry,' he said. 'It's been quite a day, hasn't it?'

'You could say that.'

'I'm phoning, Ali, because I knew you wanted to speak to me today. In all the hullabaloo, I'm afraid I didn't get round to seeing you.'

'That's OK, Harvey. Don't worry about it.'

'If you'd like to come and talk to me tomorrow— maybe after the shift might be a good time. There's less chance of being disturbed then. Is that all right, Ali?'

Just for a moment she found herself hesitating. Harvey obviously still thought she wanted to speak to him about her job, about resigning—or at least transferring to another department. Was that still what she wanted?

'Ali, are you still there?'

'Yes, yes, Harvey, I'm still here.'

'Oh, I thought we'd been cut off. So, about tomorrow. . .?'

'Harvey—' she took a deep breath '—I don't think I need to come and see you now, after all.'

There was a silence at the other end of the line, then hesitatingly he said, 'You don't. . .?'

Did he sound surprised? He'd been there when Connor had given his reasons for coming to Denehurst. Was he drawing his own conclusions?

'No,' she said, 'I've changed my mind.'

'Well, I'm glad to hear it.' The relief in his voice was obvious but then he said, 'But you seemed adamant before that you couldn't work with Dr Stevens.'

'I know,' she replied. 'But I overreacted. I've had time to think since and I realise it would be foolish giving up my job and possibly my home.'

'It's a relief to hear you say that, Ali,' said Harvey. 'On the other hand, if you want to talk. . .'

'No, Harvey,' she interrupted him quickly, 'really, there's no need.'

'I wouldn't want any friction within the team.' A note of doubt had crept into his voice.

'There won't be, I can assure you. I promise I'll behave.' She gave a short laugh.

'I wasn't meaning you,' Harvey replied quickly. 'I was thinking more of Connor Stevens. Do you want me to have a word with him, Ali?'

'That's sweet of you, Harvey. But no, it won't be necessary,'

'OK, if you're sure. Well, I won't keep you any longer. I can't bear to think of you dripping all over the carpet. See you tomorrow, Ali.'

'Yes, Harvey,' she said, 'see you tomorrow.'

Thoughtfully she replaced the receiver.

Well, she'd made her decision—burnt her bridges— so all she could do now was to get on with things. Treat Connor Stevens just like any other member of staff, forget what they had once been to each other and forget that he now loved another woman—loved her enough to want to marry her.

In spite of her newly made resolutions, it wasn't without a certain amount of apprehension that Ali went on duty the following day.

'I've put Jessica with you this morning,' said Harvey as she reached the nurses' station. 'Hopefully it'll be a little less frantic than yesterday.'

There was no mention of their conversation of the night before and Ali was grateful for that. She was still a little on edge about seeing Connor and was just wondering if he was, in fact, on duty that morning when she heard his voice coming from behind the closed curtains of a cubicle. Her heart gave a little jump at the sound, then the curtain was whisked aside and he was standing there facing her.

For a long moment they stared at each other and Ali felt as if her heart did a somersault before it settled down.

'Good morning, Connor,' she said, and was amazed at how calm her voice sounded.

'Hello, Ali,' he replied, and just for a moment she thought his eyes searched hers as if they were seeking something—some sign. Then, in the arrival of a sudden flurry of patients, the moment was gone.

Her first patient was a young girl who had been delivering newspapers before going to school and had been knocked from her bicycle by a man opening a car door without first checking that it was safe to do so.

'People in cars have no idea what it's like for poor cyclists,' said Connor as he came in to see the girl, Hayley, after Ali and Jessica had done an assessment and prepared her. 'Staff Nurse McKenzie knows though, don't you?' He glanced up at Ali as he gently examined the girl's wrist.

Ali nodded and the girl looked with interest from Connor to her and then back to Connor again.

'She cycles to work every day,' Connor smiled, 'so she'll have every sympathy with what's happened to you. Now, young lady,' he went on, sitting on the bed and earning a frown of disapproval from Ali, 'when you fell from your bike, you put your hand out to save yourself. Am I right?'

The girl nodded tearfully, her eyes never leaving Connor's face.

'Well, you probably did save yourself to a certain extent but, in doing so, I think you've broken your wrist.' Connor gently stroked the injured wrist as he spoke.

'Oh, no!' Hayley looked horrified at the prospect and her eyes filled with tears again.

'Hey, come on,' said Connor softly. 'There's nothing to worry about, you know. We'll take you down to X-Ray and make sure... Ah, here's Joe now—' he glanced up as the porter suddenly appeared '—and he's got his wheelchair; he must think it's your leg that's broken. We won't tell him—otherwise he'll make you walk.' He winked at Joe.

At that moment Hayley's mother arrived and had to be reassured that her daughter wasn't badly injured. As they went off to X-Ray, Harvey called out to Connor and asked him to go to the treatment room.

Ali turned back to the cubicle. 'Let's get cleared up in here,' she said, then realised that Jessica was still standing outside staring down the corridor. 'What's wrong?' she called.

'I think he's brilliant,' said Jessica dreamily, coming back into the cubicle.

'Who?'

'Him. Dr Stevens.'

'Oh. I see.' For one moment Ali didn't know quite what to say.

'He's marvellous with the patients,' Jessica went on. 'He's got such a way with him—a real bedside manner. He makes people relax and feel at ease.' With a sigh, she turned and began helping Ali. 'Don't you agree?' she asked after a moment when Ali remained silent.

'Well...'

'I know he hasn't been here long,' Jessica broke in enthusiastically, 'and it probably takes longer than that to really get to know someone but, well, yesterday I thought he was marvellous.'

'Yesterday certainly was an exceptional day,' agreed Ali cautiously.

'I watched him,' said Jessica. 'He was absolutely

everywhere. When he wasn't in the treatment room, he was talking to relatives—I even heard him telling a woman her husband had been killed in the crash— honestly, it can't get much worse than that, can it? I mean, there's no easy way to do that.'

'It's all part of the job, Jessica.'

'Yes, I know.' The girl sighed again. 'It gets pretty grim at times, doesn't it? And some days. . .well, some days it gets to you more than others, if you know what I mean.'

'I do know what you mean. Some days we have our own problems to cope with as well. . . Speaking of which. . .' Ali paused and looked at Jessica. . .how are things with you? Your boyfriend?'

'We've decided to cool things for a while.' A guarded look came into the girl's eyes. 'Give ourselves a break, so to speak, while we sort out what it is we both really want.'

'I think that's very wise,' said Ali. 'After all, you've got all the time in the world and, if it's meant to be, you'll get together again.'

'You sound just like my mum,' said Jessica. 'She said that.'

Not for the first time Ali wondered how old Jessica thought she was.

'This chap you lived with,' Jessica went on as they left the cubicle, 'do you still see him?'

'Sorry?' Ali threw her a startled glance. Just for the moment she had forgotten what she had told Jessica.

'You said you lived with someone for two years,' Jessica said. 'I just wondered if you still saw him.'

'Oh, no, not really,' Ali replied hurriedly, then added, 'After all, it was three years ago.'

'You mean you haven't seen him since you split up?'

'Er. . .once or twice.' Ali wondered what Jessica would say if she knew that it was Connor she had lived with, especially as the girl had just been singing his praises.

'So how did you feel?'

'What do you mean?' Ali frowned. The conversation seemed as if it could be getting out of control and, while she had no objection to giving the girl a bit of advice, she had no intention of discussing details of her relationship with Connor. To make matters worse, at that moment Connor himself appeared in the doorway of the treatment room.

'Could we have some help in here, please?' he asked as he caught sight of Ali and Jessica.

Ali nodded in reply but as they walked to the treatment room Jessica, apparently not to be thwarted, persisted with her questioning. 'Did it upset you when you saw him?'

'A bit,' Ali admitted.

'I should have thought it would have been more than a bit,' Jessica went on as they entered the room. 'After all, two years is a long time.'

'All right, yes, more than a bit,' Ali admitted.

'And was he upset? This guy you lived with?'

'I've no idea,' Ali replied briskly. By this time they were right inside the treatment room and Connor, who was bending over one of the beds, was within earshot. 'Let's see what Dr Stevens has for us this time,' she said in an effort to change the subject.

'I bet he was.' Jessica, however, seemed determined, ignoring all Ali's attempts. 'I bet he was upset. I mean, it must have been like being married—living with someone for two years. My cousin got a divorce from her husband and she says she still feels terrible when she sees him—and that was five years ago. I bet this guy felt pig-sick when he saw you again.'

To Ali's dismay Connor straightened up and, although he remained with his back to them, she had

the awful feeling he had heard Jessica's remarks. She
would hate him to think that she had been discussing
their relationship and with the youngest member of
staff. A moment later he turned and faced her and the
inscrutable expression on his face confirmed her fears.

'You wanted some help?' she asked as their eyes met.

'Yes.' He looked down at a young woman on the
bed. 'She's overdosed on paracetamol,' he said. 'We
need to do a stomach wash-out.'

The sight of the young woman, little older than herself, sobered Jessica enough to silence her questions.

'Have you seen a stomach wash-out before?' asked
Ali a few minutes later as the woman retched and
gagged, fighting furiously as they introduced the rubber
tubing into her throat and down into her stomach.

Jessica, now subdued, shook her head.

'You hold the funnel,' instructed Connor, 'while Ali
pours the fluids in.'

As the contents of the patient's stomach began to
surface Connor put them to one side, replacing the
bucket with another for the remainder. 'That needs to go
to the lab for analysis,' Connor explained for Jessica's
benefit, 'just in case she took something else that we
don't know about.'

'How do we know she took paracetamol?' asked
Jessica.

'The empty bottle was found beside her bed,' Connor
replied. 'Trouble is, we don't know how many
she took.'

'Who found her?' asked Ali, leaning forward and
stroking the woman's damp hair out of her eyes as she
continued to retch helplessly into the bucket.

'The police broke in when she didn't arrive for
work this morning,' said Connor. 'Apparently she'd
threatened this before and her workmates were worried.'

Gradually the fluid the woman was bringing up began

to run clear until eventually it was almost pure water in the bucket.

'I think we can stop now,' said Connor at last. 'If you'd like to get her cleaned up I'll come back in a while and do a blood test.' He touched the woman briefly on the shoulder and then moved away to the second bed in the treatment room, where a patient had just been brought in by the paramedics.

Ali removed the tubing from the young woman's stomach and Jessica helped her to lie back on her pillows. Ali guessed that the patient was very attractive under normal circumstances but after her recent ordeal she looked haggard—with dark circles beneath her eyes, her skin blotched and mottled and her hair lank and greasy.

'We'll soon have you feeling better,' said Jessica cheerfully, straightening the cellular blanket that covered the woman's legs.

Ali threw Jessica a warning glance, which she didn't see. 'We'll give you a nice wash,' she went on, 'and then you can comb your hair. You'll be amazed how much better you'll feel after that—'

'Piss off!'

Jessica stared at the woman who had laid her head back on the pillow and closed her eyes. 'I'm sorry,' she began, 'I thought. . .' She trailed off as at last she caught Ali's eye.

'I don't want to feel better. I don't want to be here,' said the woman through clenched teeth. The note of utter hopelessness in her voice finally silenced any further attempt the young student might have made at being helpful.

'You take the equipment to the sluice,' said Ali gently to Jessica. 'I'll finish here.'

Jessica scuttled away and Ali carried on cleaning up the patient in silence. She knew that the woman wouldn't want to hear anything she might choose to say at that particular time. Later she might want to talk to someone, but not yet. Not until she came to terms with the fact that what she had planned hadn't happened.

A short time after, Ali found a disconsolate Jessica in the nurses' station, talking to Connor.

'I don't seem to get anything right,' she was saying as Ali approached.

'You will, don't worry,' said Ali. 'A lot of it comes from experience and in learning what to expect.'

'I was just telling her the same thing,' agreed Connor.

'I just thought I would try and make her feel better, that's all,' said Jessica. 'After all, she must be feeling absolutely dreadful. . . And to even want to do that in the first place. . .'

'Do we know any details?' asked Ali.

'She left a note,' said Connor. 'Apparently her husband recently left her. . .'

'I can't imagine getting to that stage over any man,' said Jessica.

'It happens the other way as well,' observed Connor. 'A and E get their fair share of male suicide attempts for similar reasons.'

'Maybe. . .but even so. . .' Jessica shook her head as if the whole thing was beyond her.

'You'd be surprised how affairs of the heart are responsible for a large part of the anguish in the world,' said Connor, carefully avoiding Ali's eye as he spoke.

'I just wish I could stop putting my foot in it and learn to say the right thing at the right time,' said Jessica miserably.

'You will.' Connor stood up. 'When we are students we all make mistakes. We certainly made our fair share, didn't we, Ali?'

'Yes,' Ali nodded, hoping she appeared casual. 'Yes, I'm sure we did.' She knew the question had a double meaning but she refused to be drawn. She was about to move away out of harm's reach when she realised that Jessica was staring at them in amazement. First at Connor, then at her.

'Did you two know each other before?' she asked at last.

It was Connor who answered. 'Oh, yes,' he said, 'Staff Nurse McKenzie and I go back a long way. We did our training in the same hospital. . .' The old smile lurked around the corners of his mouth and the amusement was back in his eyes. 'You could say we are old friends.'

'And now you're working together again,' said Jessica.

'That's right. Now we're working together again.' Connor nodded.

'It's a small world, isn't it?' Jessica breathed.

'It is indeed,' replied Connor.

Ali knew that it could only be a matter of time before Jessica put two and two together and realised that the new CO was the man who had once shared her life. Not wanting to be around when she did, Ali fled out of the nurses' station and into the comparative sanctuary of the rest-room.

CHAPTER SEVEN

DURING the next couple of weeks things seemed to settle down for Ali, at least where her working life was concerned. Very gradually she began to accept having Connor around again, especially now that she knew he had not come to disrupt her life in any way. She had always enjoyed working with him in the past, both recognising and admiring his skill as a doctor, and she found this enjoyment rekindled in the days and weeks following his appointment.

Sometimes she had to remind herself that there was now someone else in his life, and occasionally when she thought about that she suffered a pang of regret, even though she was loath to admit it even to herself.

One evening, at the beginning of Connor's third week, Ali arranged to meet Maggie at the hospital social club. She was early and when she arrived there was no sign of Maggie. It was a warm, sunny evening and she'd chosen to walk, leaving her bicycle at home. All the windows in the club were open, allowing a breeze to filter through. Some members of staff had taken drinks outside and were sitting on the wall or on the sweep of grass that ran right down to the water meadows and the river beyond.

Ali glanced outside to satisfy herself that Maggie wasn't there and it was then that she caught sight of Connor. He was sitting on the wall, talking to two other doctors. He looked relaxed and casual in T-shirt and denims and as he threw back his head and laughed at something one of the others had said she felt her heart give its usual jolt.

He saw her and, to her dismay, immediately left the two men he was talking to and made his way into the club.

'Ali. Hi,' he said. 'Can I get you a drink?'

'I'm supposed to be meeting Maggie. . .' she said. 'Have you seen her?'

'No.' He shook his head. 'Maybe she's been delayed. No matter, you can have a drink with me while you're waiting.'

'I. . .' She was about to decline, then shrugged. What harm could there be in having a simple drink with him in the crowded club? 'Ok,' she said.

'What'll it be?' He looked pleased that she had accepted.

'Just an orange juice, please.'

She watched him as he strolled to the bar and ordered their drinks, and with a little sigh she looked round and saw an empty table in an alcove in front of one of the open windows. Crossing the room, she sat down. It had been another hectic day on A and E and she had been on her feet since early morning.

When Connor joined her she was surprised to see that he had bought himself a Coke.

'That's unusual for you, isn't it?' she asked as he set the glasses down on the table.

'I'm driving.' He sat down and lifted his glass. 'Cheers,' he said.

'That didn't use to stop you,' she observed drily then, lifting her glass of orange juice said, 'Yes, cheers,' and took a sip.

'I wasn't that bad—' he looked taken aback '—was I?'

'Yes, Connor,' she said, 'you were. You know you were,' she added pointedly.

'Well, maybe I was at that.' He caught her eye and

laughed. 'But it's like I told you before—I'm a reformed character these days.'

'I would never have believed it,' she said, eyeing him shrewdly. 'First smoking and now drinking. One wonders what else comes into this list of abstinence.'

'Oh, I haven't forsaken the alcohol entirely,' he laughed. 'A teetotal Irishman is a bit of a contradiction in terms. But I know my limits these days and I'm proud to say I stick to them.'

'This new image must all be to do with the incentive—whoever she is,' remarked Ali acidly. The moment she'd said it she wished she hadn't. The last thing she had intended was to mention his woman friend or even acknowledge her existence.

'That's true,' he replied evenly. 'There's nothing like a strong incentive, and that's a fact.' He laughed, the amusement gleaming in his blue eyes.

Ali, feeling suddenly uncomfortable, looked away. She didn't want to talk about this woman, even obliquely.

'I'm glad you decided to stay on in the job,' he said suddenly, growing serious.

Ali stiffened, her fingers tightening round her glass. It was the first time he'd made any reference to her apparent change of heart.

'I would have felt guilty if you'd left St Mark's or even A and E, come to that,' he went on. 'When I found you were working here I didn't think there was any reason why we shouldn't work amicably together.'

'Maybe I overreacted,' she replied abruptly, setting her drink down on the table and looking round the club again, wishing that Maggie would hurry up. It wasn't like her to be late.

'You have to admit,' Connor went on, 'your fears do seem to have been unfounded. In fact, I would go so far as to say that things are going well—don't you agree?'

'I suppose so. . .' Her reply was guarded; she wasn't too happy at the direction the conversation seemed to be taking.

'But, then, we always did work well together, didn't we, Ali? Couldn't live together—' he gave a short laugh '—but we worked well together.'

Where the hell had Maggie got to? Desperately she looked round again but still there was no sign of her friend.

'How are your parents these days?' Connor leaned back in his chair.

'They're very well, thank you.' She threw him a suspicious glance.

'I miss the chats I used to have with your dad,' he said reflectively and then, catching her eye, he said quickly, 'and your mum.' He grinned. 'Even if she never did quite trust me.'

'It was all that blarney you used to feed her.' Ali found herself smiling in spite of the fact that she wanted no fond memories from the past coming to the surface. 'And how is your mother?' Suddenly she felt obliged to ask, not just because he had asked after her parents but because she had been genuinely fond of his mother, Rose.

'She's well. . .getting older, of course, just like us all. She's never forgiven me, you know, for letting you slip through my fingers, as she puts it. She loved you on sight, Ali,' he said, then added, 'that time I took you home to Ireland. . .'

Ali cast her eyes around the club yet again and this time, to her relief, she caught sight of Maggie coming though the entrance.

Maggie saw them immediately and made her way across the floor to join them. 'I'm so sorry I'm late,' she said to Ali, 'but I see Connor has been looking after you.'

'What'll you have to drink?' Connor stood up.

'No, let me get this round.' Maggie glanced down at their nearly empty glasses. 'It's the least I can do. Same again?'

'Not for me, thanks.' Connor drained his glass. 'I have to go.' He glanced at his watch and Ali found herself wondering where he was going in such a hurry. Punctuality had never been a priority with him in the past, but, then, many things seemed to have changed in the last three years where Connor was concerned. This woman in his life certainly seemed to be exerting her influence in a way that she, Ali, had never quite been able to.

'How are the renovations going?' asked Maggie.

'Very well.' Connor nodded. 'The last of the plans have been passed by the council, so work can really commence now. It'll be a long job but there's plenty of time and it'll all be worth it in the end.'

'It's certainly a lovely spot down there. I remember going to the farm for eggs when I was a child,' said Maggie.

Ali looked from Connor to Maggie in bewilderment. What in the world were they talking about? Renovations? Eggs?

'Must go. See you girls tomorrow.' Connor raised his hand in farewell and then he was gone, through the club and outside into the last of the day's sunshine.

Ali watched as he walked past the open windows, heading for the hospital car park. When he had disappeared from view she turned to Maggie. 'What in the world was all that about?' she demanded.

'What do you mean?' Maggie had been about to go to the bar but she paused and looked back at Ali.

'All that about renovations—who's renovating what?'

'Oh, that,' said Maggie. 'It's the farm cottage

Connor's bought—he's doing it up. I'll just get the drinks. Yours was an orange juice, wasn't it?' Not waiting for Ali to confirm or deny the fact, Maggie sped off to the bar.

Ali stared after her in amazement. Surely she couldn't be hearing right. Connor buying a cottage? And renovating it?

'Phew, it's warm,' said Maggie as she returned a few minutes later with an orange juice for Ali and a lager and lime for herself. 'Sorry I was so late but my sister phoned just as I was coming out of the door and she went on for ages and ages—I thought I was never going to get away—and in the end I simply had to say—'

'Maggie,' Ali interrupted her in mid-flight, 'what's all this nonsense about Connor buying a cottage?'

'Oh, it's not nonsense—it's true,' said Maggie, taking a sip of her lager and wiping her top lip with her hand. 'Didn't you know? It's one of the cottages down at Langstone Farm. D'you know where I mean? There are three cottages down there. Two of them have been knocked into one. That's the one he's bought. He was telling me all about it in the canteen the other day.'

'But he lives at Greyfriars.' Ali looked bewildered.

'He does,' agreed Maggie cheerfully, 'at the moment. But he's only renting that just until the cottage is ready, then presumably he'll move in there.'

'You mean he's actually buying this cottage?'

'Oh, yes,' Maggie replied airily and then, catching sight of Ali's incredulous expression, she said, 'Is that so unbelievable?'

'Where Connor Stevens is concerned,' Ali replied tightly, 'yes, it is. He is the world's worst when it comes to responsibility or commitment of any kind. I would have thought the last thing he would do is saddle himself with a mortgage.'

'People change, Ali. . .' said Maggie mildly.

'Not that quickly, they don't,' retorted Ali. 'We're only talking about three years, for heaven's sake!'

'And circumstances change. . .'

Ali fell silent for a moment and sipped her drink, throwing Maggie a quick glance. 'What you mean is Connor's circumstances have changed because of this new woman in his life.'

'Well, yes, I suppose that is what I mean,' replied Maggie. 'Although,' she went on quickly, 'I wasn't going to put it quite like that but, yes, and I dare say her influence must have some bearing on what he's doing—especially if, as he said, he intends to marry her and this cottage will be their home.'

Ali swallowed. Suddenly she felt depressed. 'You said something about renovations,' she said after a moment.

'Yes, there's a lot to be done, apparently. Connor said that once the structural work is completed he intends doing much of it himself.'

'But he doesn't know the first thing about DIY.' Ali stared at Maggie. 'He hates anything like that. It was always me who did any decorating that had to be done in the flat. . .'

'I take it this is the same man we're talking about?' Maggie laughed and set her glass down.

'I must admit I'm beginning to wonder,' replied Ali, shaking her head in disbelief. 'Because I'm certainly finding it difficult to recognise the man I once knew from the things I've learnt about Connor since he's been here.'

'Have you been getting on all right with him?' Maggie suddenly looked curious.

'Oh, yes,' Ali replied quickly, then sighed. 'In fact, much better than I ever thought we could.'

'Don't you think that might be because you relaxed

when you knew his presence here wasn't a threat
to you?'

'I don't know,' Ali said slowly. 'I'm not really sure.
I suppose it could be that. . .'

'Did he show any surprise that you had changed your
mind and decided to stay after all?'

'He's never even mentioned it. . .'

'Really?'

'Until just now, that is.'

'So, what did he say?'

'That he was pleased I'd decided to stay on—that
he'd never intended to upset me.'

'And I'm sure he hadn't,' said Maggie thoughtfully.

They sat on in silence until Ali carefully set her glass
down and said, 'Has he mentioned this woman at all,
Maggie?'

'Woman?' Maggie seemed to be deliberately,
aggravatingly vague.

'Yes—' Ali struggled to remain patient '—the one
he says he wants to marry.'

'Oh, her.'

'Yes, has he said anything about her? Who she is,
or what she's like?'

'No, not really.' Maggie shook her head. 'At least. . .'
she hesitated.

'Yes?' Ali leaned forward slightly.

'No, it was nothing, really.'

'Go on, tell me.'

'He said she deserved the best.'

'He said what?'

'That she deserved the best and that he wanted to
give her the best. . . Sorry, Ali, you did ask.' Maggie
looked apologetic.

'Oh, don't worry,' said Ali airily. 'It means nothing
to me, I can assure you. I just feel sorry for her, that's
all. Whoever she is, she's got a lot to learn.'

'About Connor, you mean?'

'Most definitely about Connor,' replied Ali firmly.

Somehow, in front of Maggie she managed to appear nonchalant, as if this woman—the one Connor was going to marry; the one who he was to share the cottage with—really wasn't the slightest concern of hers. But later, after Maggie had given her a lift home and had driven away, she found herself wondering again.

She'd wondered at first when she'd first learnt about her but then, knowing that she and Connor had to work amicably together, she had somehow managed to push all thoughts of the woman to the back of her mind. Now, with all this talk of cottages and renovations, the curiosity was back. And what was even more infuriating was that it wouldn't seem to go away.

She wondered about this unknown woman for the rest of the evening.

Connor had told Maggie that she deserved the best.

Hadn't she, Ali, deserved the best when they had been together?

'Obviously not,' she told Boy Blue grimly as he jumped onto her lap and settled himself comfortably. Connor had taken the best from her—the very best she had to offer—but he not been prepared to give a lot of himself in return. But this woman, apparently, had something that Ali had lacked and Ali found that she was tormenting herself trying to fathom what it might be.

And the torment didn't last just that night. It crept into the next day, in spite of her giving herself a stern talking-to, and into the next and all the following days.

She would find herself wondering at the most inopportune moments, wondering and watching Connor when she didn't think he knew.

It was almost as if she was jealous—heaven forbid—

as if she could be! But whatever it was, she wished the feeling would just go away.

But, far from going away it just seemed to intensify— to such an extent that she began to try to visualise Connor and this woman together. The fact that she couldn't even conjure up an image of her did nothing to detract from the situation. On the contrary, the fact that she knew no physical details of this woman seemed to fire her imagination even further.

One day she found herself battling with just such emotions after overhearing Connor say to someone that he had become a member of the local tennis club.

No doubt she played tennis, Ali thought miserably. Probably played well, like Connor did, while she, Ali, was hardly a candidate for Wimbledon and never would be.

It was late on a Saturday afternoon and there had been a lull in the number of patients coming into A and E.

'It's too hot,' said Harvey. 'They can't even be bothered to injure themselves today.'

He'd spoken too soon, of course, for within the next few minutes they began to receive reports of an incident at the annual county show, which was being held in nearby meadows. What had at first started as a mild scuffle outside the beer tent had escalated into a full-scale brawl as two rival gangs, who had somehow gained admission to the ground and who had been drinking steadily for the best part of the day, clashed in a bitter exchange. The police had been swiftly on the scene but had been unable to prevent a number of serious injuries.

'We don't very often get this sort of thing,' said Ali to Jessica as they waited for the first of the casualties to arrive. 'It's usually the night shift who have the honour of patching people up after street fights and riots.'

'Well, I ask you,' said Maggie, 'who would expect violence and bloodshed on a warm, midsummer's afternoon at the county show? Oh, and talking of midsummer,' she added, 'don't forget the social club's summer barbeque at the end of next week. It's my turn to organise it this year so you'd better all be there.'

There were murmurings of assent from the rest of the staff as they waited for the first of the ambulances to arrive from the show ground.

'I wonder what the injuries will be like.' Jessica sounded apprehensive but she didn't have long to wait, for within ten minutes the first casualties began to arrive and it was soon apparent that several members of both gangs had been armed with Stanley knives.

'Looks like my needlework skills will be called into play,' observed Connor drily as he examined one youth whose face was slashed from temple to jaw. 'Can we have some cross-matching here, please, Ali. He's lost a lot of blood.'

When they moved back into the professional arena Ali felt more comfortable because that was where she and Connor still held their rapport. She had recently become uneasily conscious that the others on the team were only too aware of her previous relationship with the new CO. Jessica had guessed, just as Ali had thought she would, but, apart from the one occasion when she had asked Ali if it was true, she hadn't referred to the matter again.

Ali suspected that Maggie might have cautioned the student against mentioning it further. But, somehow, because the girl's silence was so uncharacteristic it became more unnerving than questions, or even teasing, might have been.

'Will I get good scars?' A heavily tattooed youth with a shaved head and thick gold earrings in both ears grinned at Ali as she cleaned up two cuts on both his cheeks.

'I shouldn't count on it,' replied Ali, dropping cotton-wool swabs into the dish that Jessica held.

'Well I 'ope I do after all this,' said the youth. 'Me mate will. He got a broken bottle shoved in 'is face.'

'Why do you do it?' asked Ali as Connor came into the cubicle.

'Wot?' asked the youth warily.

'Go round looking for trouble and starting fights?' Jessica intervened.

'Waddy'er mean? We didn't start it. They did. Oi! That hurt!' He glared at Connor as he examined one of the cuts.

'I'll give you an injection to deaden the pain,' said Connor.

'You should be ashamed of yourself!' Jessica obviously hadn't finished.

Connor threw Ali a quick glance and she moved forward, prepared to move the student out of the cubicle if necessary.

'I remember you from school.' Jessica apparently had no intention of being silenced. She stood, hands on hips, glaring down at the youth who stared back at her in sudden alarm. 'You're Matthew Jenkins. What in the world will your mother say when she finds out about today?'

'Eh?' The youth flinched as Connor administered a local anaesthetic near the largest of the cuts on his face.

'Your mother,' repeated Jessica. 'What will she think, for goodness sake?'

'Wot's me muvver got t'do wiv it?' demanded Matthew, but to Ali's amusement his gaze flickered away from Jessica in embarrassment.

'I would say your mother has everything to do with it,' retorted Jessica. 'She's a nice, respectable woman

and she certainly didn't bring you up to behave like
this. How do you think she's going to feel if you have
to go to prison?'

'Prison?' The youth jerked his head up sharply. 'Who
said anything about prison? Most we'll git is probation
tacked on to the last lot. Ow!' He yelped in pain and
glared at Connor.

'You must keep still,' said Connor calmly, 'otherwise
I can't guarantee where the needle will end up.'

'So why do you do it?' Jessica still hadn't finished,
and by some mutual, unspoken agreement, Connor and
Ali let her continue.

'Dunno, really.' Matthew raised his shoulders in a
slight shrug, careful this time not to move his face. 'Get
bored, I s'pose.'

'Don't you work?' said Jessica. Ali threw her a quick
glance and saw the firm set of the little pointed chin.

'Nah. Never 'ad a job.'

'What?' Jessica sounded appalled. 'Not since you left
school?'

The youth didn't reply. The slight shake of his head
was barely perceptible.

'Then you should be ashamed of yourself,' said
Jessica.

'Ain't no jobs,' muttered Matthew.

'That's no excuse,' retorted Jessica. 'If you can't find
work you could get yourself some qualifications or,
failing that, you could do some voluntary work. I've
no time for layabouts who sponge off the State and
who aren't prepared to do anything to improve their
condition.'

The youth remained silent, and gently Ali said,
'Jessica, could you get rid of these swabs, please?'

'What?' The girl gazed down at the soiled swabs in
the dish in her hands as if she'd never seen their like
before. Her eyes were glittering and there were two

bright spots of colour on her cheeks. She looked sharply at Ali and then at Matthew and then, without a word, she hurried from the cubicle.

'Bloody hell!' said Matthew shakily. 'Fank goodness she's gone!'

'She has a point, you know,' said Connor.

The remainder of the suturing was carried out in silence and as they finished, two uniformed policemen stepped into the cubicle to interview Matthew Jenkins.

'I'd better go and find Jessica,' said Ali as she and Connor made their way back to the nurses' station. 'She got pretty upset back there, but I was reluctant to stop her because I felt she might just do some good. He would never have listened to either of us if we'd spoken to him in that way, any more than he will listen to the police—or his mother for that matter,' she added as she followed Connor.

'But Jessica,' she went on, 'a girl he knew from schooldays—a girl who is obviously making something of her life—well, she just might get through where everyone else fails.'

'She reminds me of you,' said Connor, stopping and turning suddenly to face her—so suddenly that she almost careered into him.

'Me?' she said, taken aback and looking up into his face.

'Yes, you,' he replied softly, 'or rather how you were when you used to try to reform me.'

'Are you likening yourself to the Matthew Jenkinses of this world?' She said it lightly but she was only too aware of the sudden nearness of him. She had been close to him in the cubicle as they had worked together but this was different, quite different, intimate even.

'In a way, yes,' he said gently and, before she could prevent him, he reached out his hand and lightly, very lightly touched her cheek. 'I was a bit like that lad—

we just had different ways of expressing ourselves,
that's all. It's a good job there are girls like you and
Jessica around to get us back onto the straight and
narrow. The tragedy is when we take too long to do
anything about it.'

He lowered his hand but continued to look into her
eyes. For once the amusement wasn't there. Instead
there was another expression—one, Ali thought, which
could almost have been of regret.

CHAPTER EIGHT

ALI had been looking forward to the social club's summer barbeque. She had attended the previous one and had thoroughly enjoyed herself, but as the day approached and she found herself wondering if Connor would take his girlfriend she grew increasingly uneasy.

'I think I might give it a miss,' she said to Maggie one morning as they prepared to go on duty.

'Oh, no, you won't,' said Maggie firmly. 'I'm responsible for the organisation this year and I need all the support I can get. Besides, it'll be great—I've even arranged for a local jazz group to come along to play.'

'Well. . .' Ali was doubtful for, while she wanted to help Maggie, watching Connor with his girlfriend wasn't really her idea of a fun evening.

'I know what you're thinking,' said Maggie, 'but my ex-husband, Ted, plays in the jazz group and, if I know him, he'll have his latest groupie in tow. If he runs true to form it'll be some little moppet who looks about fifteen, so if I can swallow my pride so can you.'

There were three or four days of rainy, unsettled weather that week, during which Maggie went about with a desperate expression on her face, but the barbeque day itself dawned to an early morning mist that hovered over the river and the water meadows but which cleared by mid-morning, giving way to bright, warm sunshine.

It was Ali's day off but after lunch, clad in shorts and a white cotton shirt knotted beneath her midriff, she cycled to the hospital to see if she could give Maggie a hand with the preparations for the evening.

111

The barbeque, an annual event at St Mark's, was to be held on the field behind the hospital social club. A marquee had been erected the previous day and when Ali arrived she found the caterers setting up the barbeques, and men from the local brewery unloading crates from their delivery van and carrying them into the marquee.

The hospital porters and maintenance crew had set up a small dais beneath a red and white striped awning, ready for the jazz band, and stacks of chairs were being carried from the hospital conference room and set around groups of tables on the grass.

Maggie, in jeans and a striped T-shirt and with her auburn hair caught up on the top of her head and a clipboard in her hand, was dashing around like a demented bumble-bee issuing instructions. The moment she saw Ali she pounced.

'Good,' she said. 'I had an awful feeling you were going to chicken out of all this.'

Ali pulled a face. 'Don't tempt me,' she said but, on seeing Maggie's expression, she added, 'Relax. I'm here, aren't I?'

'True—' Maggie eyed her speculatively '—but will you be here tonight?'

'That's another matter entirely.' Ali looked round as she spoke. 'On the other hand,' she murmured after a moment, 'all this is quite infectious. I suppose it could be fun.'

'Of course it will be fun!' exploded Maggie. 'I haven't gone to all this trouble for nothing, you know.'

'I like your idea of a 1920s theme, Maggie,' said Ali with a smile and, as an afterthought, added, 'Did they have barbeques in the twenties?'

'I shouldn't have thought so,' replied Maggie flippantly. 'I had thought of making it a chicken and champagne picnic. . .but I was afraid no one would come. The barbeque has become something of a tradition at St Mark's.'

'And the beer tent,' observed Ali, as the two delivery men rolled a barrel down a ramp from the back of their van.

'Yes,' agreed Maggie, 'and the beer tent. Got your costume?' she added, turning back to Ali.

Ali nodded. 'Yes, I hired one in the end. I didn't have time to make anything.'

'From what I've heard the local hire shop has done very well,' said Maggie with a chuckle.

'So, now that I'm here, what do you want me to do?'

Maggie glanced round. 'Could you sort out all the tablecloths, serviettes and cutlery? They're in big cartons inside the club kitchen.'

'I'm on my way,' replied Ali and, with a wave of her hand, left Maggie to her lists and headed for the kitchen entrance of the club. She worked steadily unpacking the cartons and when she had finished she helped Joe, the casualty porter, to carry yet more chairs out onto the field.

Ali wished that she could raise more enthusiasm over the forthcoming event but she found that she was hard pushed to do so. Usually she was a fun person and under normal circumstances would have been eagerly looking forward to a barbeque, especially one with music and dancing and with such an enchanting theme, but all she could think of was that Connor would be there with *her*—the woman who deserved the best, as Ali had come to think of her.

She wondered what her costume would be like. She had already in her mind's eye come to the conclusion that the girl would be tall and willowy. Connor liked tall, slim girls. And she would be dark, she was fairly certain of that, and her hair, of course, would be long—not short like hers. Connor had said that he liked her

hair short, that it suited her, but she could remember
on other memorable occasions when he had told her
that he liked to see it spread across the pillow.

Oh, yes, most certainly her hair would be long.
She would be wearing something diaphanous and no
doubt very expensive, and she would be draped on
Connor's arm.

By the time she had finished helping Maggie and had
returned to her house to change, Ali was desperately
casting around for an excuse not to go. Perhaps she
could ring Maggie and say that she had a headache.
But that sounded a bit wimpish. . .a migraine sounded
better. Besides, no one had common or garden head-
aches these days, only migraines.

Yes, that was what she'd say. She was very sorry
but she had a migraine and it would be quite impossible
for her to come to the barbeque.

She'd never had a migraine before. Did one feel sick
with migraine? She thought so. Maybe she should check
up first in her nursing manual, just in case Maggie asked
what her symptoms were. She'd just feed Boy Blue first.

The cat rubbed himself affectionately round her legs
as she spooned his supper into his bowl and as he tucked
enthusiastically into his meal Ali watched him for a
moment. Then she wandered upstairs to her bedroom
to find her nursing manual.

The dress she had hired to wear for the evening was
hanging on the wardrobe door. Sleeveless and with a
plain round neckline, the soft, peach-tinted chiffon fell
from a dropped waistband into floating, handkerchief
points around the hemline. She had loved the dress on
sight and with the matching diamanté headband around
her short dark hair she had more than looked the part.

The woman in the hire shop had gone into raptures
when Ali had tried the outfit on and stepped from the
fitting-room.

'Oh, that's perfect! Quite perfect!' The woman had clasped her hands. 'I shouldn't say this, I know, but so often people choose the most inappropriate costumes and end up looking ludicrous but you, well, dear, you look as if you've stepped right out of that era.'

Ali smiled in spite of herself as she recalled the woman's enthusiasm. It was a pity she wouldn't be wearing the dress now. She would have quite enjoyed it—she'd always loved books and films about the Roaring Twenties. She lingered, fingering the soft material, and it was at that moment the phone rang.

Turning from the wardrobe, she picked up the receiver. It was Maggie.

'Ali, are you using your shoulder-bag tonight—the one with the thin chain strap?'

She took a deep breath. 'No, Maggie. In fact, I. . .'

'Oh, good. Can I borrow it, please?'

'Yes. . .but, Maggie. . .'

'You'll bring it with you, then? Thanks. Do you know, Ali,' she carried on, not giving Ali the chance to interrupt, 'I was getting quite twitchy about Ted being there, so I've just had a soak in the bath and given myself a good talking-to. I'm going to get dolled up to the nines and go and sock it to him. Make him regret what he gave up. Do you blame me?'

'Er. . .no. No, Maggie, of course not,' she said.

'It's the only way, Ali. Believe me. Life's too short for regrets. You've just got to get on with it and enjoy yourself. At least, that's the intention. So, if you see me having a quiet sob into my lager tonight, I want you to haul me back onto the dance floor. Can I rely on you for that?'

'Yes, Maggie.' She was laughing now. 'Yes, of course you can.'

She was still smiling when she replaced the receiver.

Then, with a sigh, she turned and looked at the peach dress.

She deliberately arrived fairly late, when the barbeque was well under way, in the hope that she would be absorbed into the crowd and somehow become, if not entirely invisible, at least inconspicuous.

The field was crowded not only with members of staff and their partners but with past patients who had joined the hospital's League of Friends. Most had entered into the spirit of the occasion and were dressed in 1920s attire, the girls in flapper dresses and headbands or cloche hats, and the men in striped blazers and flannels—a few even sporting straw boaters.

Clutching a plastic cup of sparkling cider, Ali stood and looked around her apprehensively. To her relief, there was no sign of Connor. Maybe he had decided not to come after all. Ali felt herself relax a little.

An appetising smell wafted across the field from the barbeque grills, where the team of caterers in blue and white striped aprons and tall chef's hats charcoaled juicy steaks, chicken legs and succulent strips of pork.

The members of the jazz band were assembling on the dais and little snatches of music drifted across the heads of the crowd as they warmed up.

'Ali, you look divine!'

She turned sharply and found Maggie behind her. She grinned. 'You don't look so bad yourself.' Maggie's very short dress was of white satin with sequined shoulder-straps. Her stockings were white, the toes of her shoes very pointed and in her jewelled headband she wore a blue plume. She had teased her auburn hair into a cluster of curls that framed her face and the overall effect was quite enchanting. The finishing touch was supplied by the shoulder-bag Maggie had requested.

'Not exactly barbeque attire, though, is it?' Maggie

pulled a face. 'Last year's Wild West theme was far more appropriate.'

'But nowhere near as original. . .' Ali broke off as the jazz band suddenly swung into its first number and every head in the crowd turned towards the dais.

'That was a stroke of genius, getting them here.' Ali raised her voice so that Maggie could hear.

'Maybe. I hope I don't live to regret it.'

'You said no regrets. Remember?'

Maggie smiled.

'Which one is Ted, by the way?' Ali asked after a while.

'The little tubby guy at the back playing the saxophone.'

'He isn't tubby,' said Ali mildly.

'Yes, he is,' said Maggie, 'and balding, but he thinks he's still twenty-five, slim and virile.' She glanced round as she spoke. 'Good crowd here. Have you had anything to eat yet?'

'No.' Ali shook her head. 'I will in a minute. I'm enjoying the music at the moment. They're good, aren't they?'

Maggie nodded, then said with a sigh, 'I suppose I'd better go and make sure the raffle is under way.'

'Want any help?'

'No, thanks, I've got Gareth Morgan and his mob from Paediatrics running it this year. You stay and enjoy yourself. I'll see you later.'

Maggie moved away and Ali turned her attention back to the band. They really were very good and were already claiming the attention of a large section of the crowd. So immersed did she become in the catchy strains of the rhythm that she jumped at the sudden voice in her ear.

'Wonderful, this re-creation of history, isn't it?'

She turned to find Connor beside her.

'But for history to really repeat itself,' he carried on, not giving her a chance to answer, 'I would need to tip a glass of beer down your back.'

For a moment she could think of nothing to say.

'Even the circumstances are the same,' he added. 'I seem to remember that was a barbeque as well.'

Still she floundered for something to say. His allusion to their first meeting had floored her completely.

'We did manage to sponge the beer out of that top you were wearing, if I remember rightly. We might not be so lucky this time.' His gaze travelled admiringly over the peach dress. 'You look beautiful, Ali,' he said softly at last.

She turned away in confusion. This was not what she had envisaged at all. She had almost steeled herself for seeing him with his girlfriend, but she certainly wasn't prepared for him to stand there whispering compliments into her ear.

'Are you on your own?' she asked and, because she was nervous, the words came out more sharply than she had intended.

Connor glanced around him, an amused expression on his face. 'I think so,' he said. 'I don't see anyone else.'

'What I meant was,' she said, feeling suddenly foolish, 'did you come on your own?'

'Yes,' he nodded. 'Did you?'

'Yes.' A wary note crept into her voice as his expression changed.

'Good. In that case, I suggest we keep each other company.'

'I'm not sure that's a good idea. . .' she began.

'Nonsense. It's an excellent idea. I'm on my own this evening and so are you. It's an obvious solution. Have you eaten yet?'

'No, but. . .'

'Then I propose we head for the food before it all goes. Come on.'

To her acute dismay he took hold of her hand and began drawing her through the crowd. This was even worse than she had feared. If he had been there with his girlfriend she had already worked out that she could have avoided them, but this was different. She hadn't been prepared for this. She didn't want to go with him. Didn't want to spend the evening with him.

But it seemed that Connor had other ideas and in the end Ali had no choice, for the grip on her hand was tight and he only released her when they reached the line of chefs behind the mobile barbeque grills.

She watched him as he joked with the chefs and ordered their food. He, too, had entered into the spirit of the occasion and was wearing blazer and flannels. He reminded Ali of an upper-class Oxford undergrad of the twenties era, and her mind drifted to boating parties on the river and summer picnics on long, lazy days. The nostalgic images were surprisingly stimulating and when he returned to her side with platefuls of food and smiled down at her, she was forced to look away quickly.

'Let's go over there.' He nodded towards a band of trees that formed the boundary of the field and the water meadows beyond. The sun was sinking, only a crimson arc visible now, and the shadows beneath the trees looked cool and inviting.

She hesitated for only a moment. 'No,' she replied quickly, 'I want to listen to the music.' They could have heard the music from beneath the trees but, pleasant as it would have been, she didn't dare even entertain the idea.

'Fair enough,' Connor shrugged and, still carrying the food, followed her as she led the way back to the groups of people sitting at tables around the dais.

As they wended their way through the crowd someone called Connor's name. He stopped and both he and
Ali looked round and saw Beth sitting at a table with
her husband, Rory.

'Come and join us,' she called.

'OK, thanks.' Connor set the plates down on the table
and drew up a chair for Ali. She thankfully put down
the two drinks she had been carrying and sat down.

'Ali, you look absolutely exquisite,' said Beth,
'doesn't she, Rory?'

'She certainly does,' agreed Rory. 'Can I take this
blazer off now?'

'Well, I'm certainly taking mine off,' said Connor
with a grin. 'I would say we've more than fulfilled our
obligation.'

'We can always put them on again if Maggie
appears,' laughed Rory. 'She's taken this whole thing
so seriously—I'd be afraid to upset her.'

'You have to admit, though,' said Ali, 'it's a wonderful atmosphere. I'm glad I came.'

'Was there a chance you might not have done?'
Connor draped his blazer over the back of his chair and
sat down again.

'I had thought twice about it,' admitted Ali, avoiding
his eye as she knew he was watching her.

'It's not everyone's cup of tea, this dressing-up lark,'
said Rory. 'I must admit I wasn't too sure about
coming.'

'The only reason you didn't want to come was
because you'd miss the rugby on the telly,' sniffed Beth.

'You don't happen to know the score, do you?' Rory
looked sheepishly at Connor.

'England had just scored when I came out,' said
Connor with a grin.

They all laughed, Ali felt herself relax, and the easy
tone set the pace for the rest of the evening.

Shadows lengthened, stars appeared overhead and people began dancing. Ali smiled to herself as she caught sight of Joe dancing with Jessica. The girl looked flushed and happy, happier than Ali had ever seen her. She looked round for Maggie, but there was no sign of her friend. Ali hoped that she wasn't wallowing in misery over Ted in some corner. She glanced at the dais as she thought of Ted and at that precise moment he swung into a saxophone solo, the rest of the band falling back to give him centre stage.

Something stirred in Ali's memory and she glanced round, only to find that Beth and Rory had got up and were dancing, and before she knew what was happening Connor leaned forward from behind her and rested his chin on her shoulder.

'If we're going to complete this history-repeating-itself thing tonight, I would say that's our cue, wouldn't you?' he murmured in her ear.

Mechanically, as if her body were on autopilot, she stood up and, with Connor's hand beneath her elbow, they made their way to the fringe of the dancers.

Without a word he drew her into his arms and as Ted's sax wailed its haunting melody, with a deep sigh she rested her head against his shoulder and there she found peace—the peace a traveller found on reaching home after a long, arduous journey.

He held her gently at first, the pressure from his arms barely perceptible, but then as he lowered his head and his cheek brushed hers his grip tightened and, in the sudden rush of feeling that followed, to Ali it was as if they'd never been apart. The feel of his body against hers, the male scent of him and the tenderness of his touch were so familiar that it seemed as if the long months and years of their separation had never been.

'Wasn't it this tune,' he murmured at last, 'that we

danced to all those years ago at that barbeque on the night we met?'

'Yes,' she breathed, 'yes, it was.'

'If only one could put the clock back. . .'

'That's impossible. . .'

'I know. . . Ah, I know. . .'

For one moment she could have sworn that there was a note of regret in his voice as he drew her even closer.

Ali danced most of the time after that—with Rory, once with Harvey, even with Francis Braithwaite, who graced the proceedings with a brief appearance and who told her that she looked utterly enchanting and reminded him of a photograph of his mother in her youth, and then again and again she danced with Connor.

At one point she thought that she should resist; refuse him perhaps once at least; that this could be dangerous; had been just what she had been afraid of when he had come back into her life. Then, seduced by the atmosphere, the music and possibly a touch of midsummer madness, she gave up the attempt.

All the old memories and sensations were evoked as inhibitions melted away. They had known each other so well once—every mood, every expression, every inch of each other's bodies and just what it took to please each other. It had been, Ali thought as they swayed gently together, just as Jessica had once observed—as if they had been married. Only they hadn't been married. . .there had not been enough commitment in the end and the relationship had fallen apart. Would it have been any different if they had been married? Or would they simply have become divorce statistics?

Her head began to spin and she didn't know whether it was from the effects of the cider or simply from the excitement of being close to Connor. Once again she rested her head on his shoulder. Whether or not they would have stayed together if they had been married was something they would now never know because. . . because Connor was going to marry someone else.

She dismissed the thought almost as soon as it entered her head. She didn't want to think about that tonight. She'd thought about little else recently and she knew that come tomorrow it would be back.

But for now, during this night—a night of summer madness, call it what you will—she didn't want to think; she just wanted to enjoy the pleasure of being in his arms again.

'Can I see you home?' he asked when the evening was almost over and people were drifting away.

'Well. . . I. . .'

'I promise I'll behave myself.'

She giggled. She wasn't sure that she wanted him to behave himself.

'I take it you didn't cycle. . .?' he said, misinterpreting her mirth.

'No,' she laughed, 'I didn't cycle. I took a taxi.'

'So did I,' he admitted. 'How about we walk back to your place along the tow-path? The moonlight should ensure we don't end up in the river.'

She knew that she should refuse. Knew that it was lunacy to go with him, but it was as if all her powers of reasoning and resistance had evaporated into the soft night air.

She even made no objection when he took her hand and together they strolled, Connor with his blazer slung over one shoulder and she carrying her heeled shoes, out of the field and away from the hospital grounds and the last of the revellers, ducking beneath the dark branches of the boundary trees then out onto the tow-path, bright with moonlight.

The last poignant strains of music followed them across the meadows and floated downstream while they

walked in silence, a silence born from a deep under-
standing of each other.

When they reached a stile halfway along the tow-path
Connor climbed over first and then as Ali took his hand
he stepped forward so that, as her feet touched the
ground, she almost fell into his arms.

Still she offered no resistance, even when his mouth
sought and then found hers. Tomorrow would be soon
enough for regrets, for recriminations—tonight an inde-
finable magic prevailed.

His kiss was just as she remembered and every bit
as wonderful, both tender and exciting as he aroused
long-forgotten desires. Her response was spontaneous,
her arms curling around his neck, her fingers sinking
into the thick dark hair and her lips parting to
receive him.

This magic, she knew, was being rekindled purely
for old times' sake, just as Connor knew it, so surely
as long as they both understood that no harm could
come from it.

The kiss lasted a long time and just as passions began
to simmer dangerously and arousal reached danger
levels for them both, a sound in the trees alongside the
path startled them and they drew apart.

'It's an owl,' said Connor shakily and they both
watched as the large bird flapped sedately across the
river, through the water meadows on the far bank and
into a distant belt of trees.

The owl had interrupted the intensity of their passion
and as they at last walked on in silence Ali wondered
what would happen when they reached her house. No
doubt Connor would expect her to invite him inside,
but if she did she knew what would happen. She had
found it hard enough before to resist him; to pretend
that he meant nothing to her any more. Now, after the
evening they had just spent and the kiss they had just

shared, she knew that would be impossible.

At the same time her common sense struggled to get the upper hand, telling her how bitterly she would regret it the next day if she allowed him to make love to her again.

Maybe, temptation urged, she could treat it purely for what it was—two people enjoying a revival of something that had once been between them; something that was over really; something that could never, ever be allowed to happen again.

The church tower suddenly loomed on the horizon and as they left the towpath she made her decision. Let tonight happen, purely for old time's sake, in memory of what they had once been to each other, then maybe she could exorcise the ghost of their relationship once and for all.

Her nerves were stretched to breaking point by the time they reached her front door. Turning the key in the lock she half turned to Connor. 'Coffee?' she said as the door swung open and she walked into the hall.

He didn't answer and she thought that he had followed her. When she turned, however, he was still standing on the threshold.

'Aren't you coming in?' She tried to keep the surprise from her voice.

'No, Ali,' he said quietly, 'I don't think that would be a good idea,' and, leaning towards her, he gently kissed the tip of her nose. 'I promised you I would behave myself and if I come in we both know I won't keep that promise.'

Then, to her amazement, he turned and walked quickly away, his footsteps echoing in the midnight silence of Church Close.

CHAPTER NINE

ALI shut the front door and found that she was shaking. Connor had gone. But wasn't that what she would have expected him to do? Slowly she walked through the hall into her sitting-room. When she had left the house that evening she hadn't even wanted to go to the barbeque, let alone have Connor bring her home.

But that had been then. And this was now. That had been before she'd known that he was going to be on his own that evening; before he had told her she looked beautiful; before he'd danced with her and held her close. And before he'd kissed her.

She stood at the French doors, staring out at the stillness in the moonlit square beyond. Her heart was still racing. What in the world was wrong with her? She was behaving like a teenager after her first date. Why, even Jessica would have more sense than this.

She had been so adamant all along, so sure she would not succumb to Connor's charm again, and yet here she was—one kiss and she'd been ready to tumble into bed with him again.

But had she? Would she actually have done that?

Abruptly she turned away from the window. Was that all it had been, Connor's charm at work again? That old charm that she should be well used to by now; the old charm that had always melted her heart and seen her taking him back after yet another episode of outrageous behaviour.

Deep down she knew that it hadn't only been that; deep down she knew that she had enjoyed being with him again; had enjoyed his attention and his flattery.

She had loved being in his arms again. It had felt so right, as if somehow it was where she belonged, and when he had kissed her there was no way that she could pretend it had been one-sided because her response had been completely spontaneous. And if he had come in with her she would have wanted him to make love to her.

As it was he had gone, leaving her with a desire deep inside that ached for release.

In the cold, clear light of day, when her head was clear, things looked different, as they usually did. She lay in bed, staring at the ceiling. Had all that really happened the night before? Had she really been prepared to put herself right back at square one where Connor was concerned? If she had and he, too, had been prepared for that to happen, he would be lying here beside her now.

Turning her head, she looked at the empty space, just as she had done so many times in the past three years since Connor had gone out of her life and she had allowed no other man in.

And suddenly she was glad that it hadn't happened. Things were different now from what they had been before because Connor was practically engaged to be married, and Ali knew that if she carried on down this particular road it would lead to yet more heartbreak.

As it was, she could go to work the next day and treat the evening for what it had been—a nostalgic, light-hearted episode between two old friends who had attempted to recapture a little magic from the past.

She had only been at work on Monday morning for a short while, however, before it became blatantly obvious that even if she was prepared to dismiss the events of the evening in that way, there were others who quite definitely weren't. . .

Beth was the first. 'I say,' she said as she and Ali

met in the corridor, 'what happened to you and Connor at the end of the barbeque?'

'Well, you and Rory were still dancing. . .' Ali began.

'When we got back you two had gone!'

'Sorry, we. . .'

'I said to Rory—' Beth obviously wasn't going to let the matter drop '—they could have waited to say goodbye. . .'

'Well—' Ali knew some sort of explanation was going to be necessary '—you see, we decided to. . .'

'And Rory said,' Beth continued, not giving her any chance to explain, 'you quite obviously had other things on your mind.'

'. . .walk home. . .' Ali finally managed to conclude, then, 'Oh!' she exclaimed as she realised what Beth had said. 'I don't know what you're talking about,' she added, staring indignantly at her.

'Oh, come on, Ali!' Beth snorted. 'I wasn't born yesterday, you know. You two were all over each other on the dance floor!'

'We were not!' Embarrassed, Ali glanced over her shoulder. Harvey was standing at the entrance to the nurses' station but, to her relief, there was no sign of Connor.

'Yes, you were,' said Beth. 'Both Rory and I commented on it. In fact, I said to Rory afterwards that if I didn't know better I would have said you two knew each other very well indeed. Rory said was I sure you didn't, and I said that you couldn't because Connor had only just come to St Mark's.'

'That's absolutely right,' said Ali, recovering something of her equilibrium.

It wasn't that easy, however, to get one over on Beth for she frowned and said, 'On the other hand, maybe you knew each other before Connor came here. . .'

Mercifully Ali was saved from answering as Harvey

called her at that moment and, without a backward glance, she hurried away from a bemused Beth. For one moment she half expected Harvey to make some comment but he didn't. Instead, he told her of a patient who had just arrived and who was in one of the cubicles with Jessica.

'She's scalded her arm and hand with boiling water,' he said. 'She's got it under running cold water and I'm allowing Jessica to get a history and do an assessment. See what she's come up with.'

She had begun to move away when Harvey, who had been about to go back into the station, paused. 'You all right, Ali?' he asked casually.

His manner was almost too casual and she replied quickly, 'Yes, yes, thank you, Harvey,' and then bolted, not giving him a chance to even ask if she'd had a good time at the barbeque. Probably he hadn't been going to say anything of the sort, she told herself firmly. She was just getting paranoid after Beth's observations.

She took a deep breath before going into the cubicle, only to find that if Beth's and Harvey's attitudes towards the events of the previous Saturday evening had presented a problem then Jessica's was something else entirely. The girl's eyes were positively shining as she looked up at Ali.

'It was wonderful, wasn't it?' she said, as if seeking reassurance from someone that what she was referring to hadn't been a dream or a figment of her imagination.

'Er. . .what?' Ali's gaze flickered from Jessica to the patient, a young woman of perhaps thirty who was sitting beside the wash basin, her forearm and hand held under the cold running tap.

'The other evening,' said Jessica in apparent amazement that someone who had actually been there could even doubt to what she was referring. 'The barbeque!'

'Oh, the barbeque!' Ali caught the patient's eye and

they both smiled at the student's enthusiasm. 'Yes, it was very good. Now, Jessica, tell me what we have, please.'

For one moment Jessica looked bewildered and then her face cleared. 'Oh, yes,' she mumbled, 'right. This is Caroline Watson. She was making a pot of tea this morning when the kettle suddenly bubbled and she tipped the water all over her left hand and arm. Harvey—sorry, Charge Nurse Gatten—instructed me to provide cooling to the scalded area to reduce the heat, to relieve pain and to prevent further tissue damage.'

'Good. Well done, Jessica,' said Ali. 'Now, I'll prepare a saline dressing which we can apply to the scalded area.' She turned to the patient. 'This will keep the area cool until the doctor comes and examines it and decides on any further treatment or dressings.

'We have to take great care there is no risk of infection,' Ali said as she prepared the saline dressing. Glancing up at Jessica and noticing how subdued the girl had become, she said, 'So you enjoyed yourself on Saturday, then?'

'Oh, yes.' The girl looked up quickly. 'I had a lovely time.'

'That wouldn't have had anything to do with a certain member of the portering team by any chance, would it?' asked Ali.

'It may have done.' Jessica flushed.

Carefully Ali applied the dressing to the patient's hand and arm, noticing as she did so that large, fluid-filled blisters had already formed.

'Hmm,' she said, 'the doctor will be along in a minute to look at those.'

'You seemed to be having a pretty good time yourself,' said Jessica casually, not taking her eyes from the patient's injuries.

'It was a lovely evening,' agreed Ali guardedly, then

at the sound of footsteps outside the cubicle she found
that she was steeling herself to face Connor. She hadn't
seen him since that moment on her doorstep, and all
kinds of emotions seemed to be chasing each other
around in her brain. She glanced up as the curtain was
whisked aside, expecting to meet those incredibly blue
eyes, but instead of Connor it was Samara who stood
there, white coat open over her saffron-coloured sari.

She was disappointed. There was no denying that.
Not only had she been expecting to see him, she realised
with a sudden, delicious thrill, she had actually been
looking forward to it.

'Good morning.' Samara gave her customary nod.

'Good morning, Doctor.' Ali recovered quickly.
'This lady, Miss Watson, has scalded her left arm and
hand with boiling water. The scalds have been cooled
and we've applied a saline dressing.'

'Is there blistering of the skin?' asked Samara.

'Yes, Doctor,' replied Jessica. 'On two fingers, across
the back of the hand and on the forearm.'

'Let me see, please,' said Samara.

Gently, with tweezers, Ali lifted the saline dressing
that was keeping the wounded areas clean and Samara
leaned forward to examine them.

'I think,' said Samara at last, 'de-roofing of the blisters, then Flamazine cream and a light gauze dressing.
You be better soon.' She smiled at the patient, who was
beginning to look very nervous, and then with another
nod at Ali and Jessica she left the cubicle.

Ali watched her go. Connor quite obviously wasn't
on duty that morning. Maybe it was just as well, she
thought as she turned back to the patient. The more
time that passed between their last meeting and the next
could only be for the better.

'What in the world is de-roofing?' asked Caroline
Watson fearfully. 'It sounds horrendous, like something

that shouldn't happen outside the building trade.'

'Don't worry.' Ali laughed. 'It's nowhere near as bad as it sounds and I promise you you'll feel a lot more comfortable afterwards. We'll leave you to rest for a few minutes while we go and set up the dressing trolley. Come on, Jessica,' she added to the student. Together they left the cubicle and went to the rear of the nurses' station.

'I'm not sure about de-roofing either,' said Jessica.

Ali threw her a quick glance and noticed that the girl looked almost as nervous as the patient. 'I'll explain,' she said, 'while we're setting up the trolley. You get the dressing packs.'

'All that de-roofing really means,' she went on when Jessica returned with the dressing packs from the stores, 'is that we cut away the tops of the blisters. This helps the healing process in that no further fluid is allowed to accumulate under the skin. Then we apply Flamazine cream and a gauze dressing.'

'Just one dressing?' asked Jessica.

'No.' Ali shook her head. 'We'll dress the fingers individually—that will prevent adhesions developing between them. When the dressings are complete we'll apply a light gauze bandage to hold them in place.'

'Won't the cutting of the blisters increase the risk of infection?'

'No,' Ali replied. 'We take our time and, needless to say, every instrument we use is completely sterile.' As she finished speaking she turned to wheel the trolley from the station and almost collided with Maggie, who was coming in. 'Whoops, sorry, Maggie,' she said. 'Didn't see you there.'

Normally there would have been some light-hearted quip from Maggie but this morning she seemed strangely subdued, only acknowledging Ali with the briefest of nods.

'Maggie?' Ali stopped and looked round but Maggie had her back to her and was scanning the shelves as if searching for a particular dressing. 'Maggie,' she repeated, 'are you OK?'

She did turn then but when Ali fully caught sight of her face she could see that Maggie most definitely wasn't OK. She was white and there were dark circles under her eyes as if she hadn't slept very well.

'I'm fine,' she muttered wearily.

'You don't look it,' said Ali.

'Thanks, Ali, for those kind words,' said Maggie with a grimace. 'I feel really good now.'

'I'll see you in the canteen at lunchtime,' said Ali briskly.

'Well. . .'

'No buts. Canteen. Lunchtime.'

Maggie nodded and turned back to the shelves and Ali pushed the trolley on out of the station and down the corridor to where Jessica was waiting for her.

By the end of the morning Ali was forced to admit that she missed Connor. She missed his presence on the unit as a doctor and she missed his personality and wit about the place, but most of all she missed Connor the man.

She hadn't realised just how used to him she had become in the last few weeks and now that she stopped to think about it, she was amazed that she could have gone from actively not wanting to work with him to actually missing him when he wasn't there.

Throughout the morning she had also found herself wondering about Maggie and what could be wrong with her. Because Connor was so much on her mind, her thoughts automatically turned to the barbeque and she wondered if Maggie's problem could be anything to do with her ex-husband, Ted.

At last Harvey released the two of them to go to

lunch and they made their way to the staff canteen.

Ali chose pasta and salad from the self-service bar and Maggie some ham sandwiches. It wasn't until they were settled at a window table and were at least a third of the way through their lunch that Ali managed to bring the conversation round to what was wrong with Maggie. Until then Maggie had kept up non-stop chatter about nothing in particular, almost as if she didn't want Ali to question her.

'So come on, then,' Ali said at last, setting down her knife and fork, 'are you going to tell me?'

'Tell you what?' Maggie took a mouthful of her sandwich and began chewing steadily.

'What it is that's bothering you,' replied Maggie patiently.

'What makes you think there is anything bothering me?' Maggie raised one eyebrow but carried on chewing.

'I've got to know you pretty well since we've been working together,' said Ali, 'and I would go so far as to say that I know when there's something bothering you.'

'And you think that's the case now, eh?' Maggie managed a faint smile.

'Let's just say you've lost your sparkle and that just isn't like you. You were all right on Saturday so something must have happened between then and now.'

When Maggie remained silent, Ali leaned across the table. 'Is this anything to do with Ted?' she asked at last.

'Ted?' Maggie looked faintly alarmed. 'Why should you think that? What's Ted got to do with anything?'

'Well, I don't know.' Ali shrugged helplessly. 'I just wondered, that's all. Ted was there, after all, at the barbeque and you did seem to be a bit on edge about that. . .'

'Did I?' Maggie looked up sharply.

'Yes, Maggie you did,' Ali replied. 'You know you

did. You said if you could cope with Ted being there with some groupie in tow, then I should be able to cope with Connor being there with his girlfriend.'

Maggie smiled faintly at that. 'Yes, I did, didn't I?' she said, then added, 'And did you?'

'Did I what?' Ali frowned.

'Cope with Connor?'

'Yes, I did, as a matter of fact, and as it happened his girlfriend wasn't there. He was on his own.'

'Really?' A flicker of interest came into Maggie's eyes.

'But it's you we're discussing, not me,' said Ali firmly as the conversation threatened to spiral right out of control. Again Maggie didn't comment, so this time Ali put her elbows on the table and said, 'So you're saying you had no problem with Ted?'

'No more than usual.' Maggie shrugged then, catching Ali's eye, she admitted, 'Oh, it does get to me when Ted's around, but I cope with it.'

'Then what? Come on, Mags, I want to know and you're not leaving this table until you tell me.'

Maggie stared at her and suddenly her shoulders sagged. 'I didn't want to tell anyone. At least not until. . .not until. . .' She took a deep breath, 'Oh, what the hell! I've found a lump,' she said.

'A lump?' Ali stared at her. She wasn't sure what she had been expecting to hear but it certainly wasn't that.

'Yes, here.' Maggie touched the side of her right breast.

Ali took a deep breath. 'So what have you done about it?' she asked briskly.

'Nothing yet.' Maggie shrugged but her casual attitude didn't fool Ali. 'I only found it yesterday morning,' she went on after a moment, 'and that was quite by chance when I was soaping myself in the shower.'

'Right, so what are you going to do about it?'

'I suppose I shall have to see someone. . .' Maggie trailed off uncertainly.

'You suppose right,' said Ali firmly. 'Do you want to see someone here or would you rather go to your GP?'

Maggie hesitated. 'I think my GP.'

'I'll come with you after work.'

'Oh, steady on.' Maggie looked up sharply. 'I don't think there need be that much haste. . .'

'I said I'll come with you after work,' repeated Ali firmly.

'Oh, all right,' Maggie muttered, 'if you say so.'

'Yes.' Ali pushed her plate away and stood up. 'I do say so.'

Maggie was on her mind for the rest of the afternoon. It didn't stop her thinking about Connor entirely, but it didn't alter the fact that she was very concerned about her friend. There was a very good chance that the lump she had found would be nothing more sinister than a harmless cyst or a small benign tumour, as Ali very well knew the majority of breast lumps were.

There was, of course, always the chance it could be something serious but even in that event, Ali told herself firmly, if it was caught early enough there was still a great deal that could be done.

When their shift was finally over the two girls travelled together in Maggie's car into Denehurst and parked in the main shoppers' car park behind the High Street. The fine spell of weather they had been enjoying for the last couple of days looked as if it might well be at an end. Low clouds had been building up all day and as they walked the short distance from the car park to the surgery the first few spots of rain began to fall.

The waiting-room was full and as Maggie was being seen as an emergency she was told that she would have to sit and wait until all the appointments were cleared.

'Home from home, isn't it?' she said, turning to Ali from the receptionist's desk. 'It could take hours.'

'That's OK,' said Ali as they sat down.

'I feel dreadful taking up your time,' Maggie protested after a few minutes.

'Don't be silly,' said Ali. 'It doesn't matter; really, it doesn't.'

'Even so,' Maggie said dubiously, 'you've had a long day.'

'So have you.' Ali grinned then, seeing that Maggie still looked concerned, she said, 'Tell you what, I've a few bits of shopping I need from the supermarket. I'll nip over there now and come back here for you. Will that make you feel better?'

'Fine.' Maggie looked relieved and Ali left her thumbing through a pile of *Country Life* magazines.

She hurried out of the surgery and into the High Street, where she crossed the road to the busy supermarket. She bought some salad and peaches for herself, a piece of coley for Boy Blue, a bottle of shampoo and some washing-up liquid. She paid at the checkout and left the store, absent-mindedly wondering if Maggie had been seen yet.

The few spots of rain they had felt earlier had turned to a steady drizzle. Dressed only in shirt and leggings and with no jacket or umbrella, Ali pulled a face as she glanced up at the sky, knowing that she would get quite wet even if she ran the short distance back to the surgery.

It was as she was waiting on the kerb to cross the road that she caught sight of a familiar car. With an almost sickening thud of excitement she realised that it was Connor's car, that it was he who was driving and that, although he was on the opposite side of the road, he was travelling towards her.

Even as she watched he slowed down, then drew in

and stopped the car by the side of the kerb. She felt surprised because he was some distance away and she didn't think he could have seen her yet.

She glanced up and down the road but she was still unable to cross because there was no break in the traffic. As she waited impatiently for the traffic to pass she saw Connor lean across the passenger seat and open the door. The next moment a figure holding an open umbrella ran out of a shop doorway and across the wide pavement to the waiting car. She folded the umbrella, shook it, got into the car and shut the door behind her.

The indicator on Connor's car flashed and as he pulled out into the traffic Ali instinctively stepped back so that he wouldn't see her.

He was laughing as the car passed her, no doubt at something his woman passenger had said, so it was unlikely that he would have seen anyone standing on the far pavement.

And, Ali thought, she was probably the last person he would have expected to see. Idiotically she found herself wondering what he would have done if he had seen her. Maybe raised his hand in greeting? Not stopped, certainly. Not with his girlfriend with him, for quite suddenly Ali knew that that was who his passenger had been.

She had only caught a glimpse of her, but it had been enough. She was young, slim, attractive and blonde. That had surprised her, she had to admit—Connor usually preferred tall brunettes.

At last there came a break in the traffic and she managed to cross. By this time she was quite wet and her hair was sticking to her head. As she passed the shop doorway from where the woman had run to Connor's car she glanced up at the sign, only to find that it was a hair salon. No wonder she'd been in a hurry if she'd just had her hair done, Ali thought grimly, catching sight of her own unbecoming appearance in the darkened shop window.

Well, she thought as she made her way back to the surgery, she'd seen her now; this woman whom Connor was going to marry. It had been inevitable really, especially in such a small town as Denehurst, that she should see her sooner or later.

So why did she suddenly feel depressed? She wasn't really sure. Maybe it was because until that moment this woman had somehow not been real, almost as if because she hadn't seen her she somehow didn't exist.

Well, Ali thought angrily, that would teach her not to be so stupid, and at the same time it put paid to any foolish notions she might have been harbouring in the last couple of days.

It had been quite ridiculous carrying on the way she had, first wallowing in nostalgia at the barbeque and afterwards during that walk home in the moonlight, and then, as if that hadn't been bad enough, even missing Connor when he wasn't at work and looking forward to seeing him again. It just served her right, seeing him with that woman.

She marched up the steps to the surgery and pushed open the doors. The trouble was they had looked so happy. . . And Ali remembered only too well that once she and Connor had been happy like that.

She looked round the waiting-room but there was no sign of Maggie. 'Has Mrs Hoskins gone in?' she asked, leaning across the reception desk.

The girl glanced at her list and nodded. 'She's with the doctor now.'

'Thanks.' Ali sat down. Suddenly she longed to tell Maggie. To pour it all out. To have Maggie sympathise with her and tell her she knew just how she felt.

But ten minutes later, when the door to the doctor's

consulting-room opened and Maggie appeared, one look at her friend's face was enough to tell Ali that her own problems would have to wait.

CHAPTER TEN

'So what happened? What did he say?' They had walked in silence from the surgery to the car park and were sitting in Maggie's car. The rain had progressed from a heavy drizzle and now spattered noisily on the roof of the car.

'I think he thought it was a cyst to start with,' said Maggie slowly at last. 'He attempted to aspirate it.'

'And?' said Ali hopefully.

Maggie shook her head and bit her lip, and Ali knew that her friend was close to tears.

'So what did he suggest?' She tried to keep her voice calm and matter-of-fact but her professional brain had gone into overdrive and she was not really surprised by Maggie's reply.

'He's arranging for me to see a consultant. . . Tim Bartholomew, he said. . .'

'He's the best, Mags. . .'

'I know. . .'

They fell silent, watching the rapidly forming puddles in the car park.

'Come on, Maggie,' said Ali at last and, reaching out, she took her friend's hand and squeezed it tightly. 'Everything will be all right. I know it will.'

Maggie had turned her face away but she looked back now and Ali saw the bright gleam of tears in her eyes. 'The number of times we say that to others,' she said, 'but it's a different matter when you're the one it's happening to. It's strange, you know. . .' she gave a deep sigh '. . .but I feel so alone. . .'

'You aren't alone, Maggie,' Ali interrupted quickly.

'I shall be there for you, and you have your family and friends at the hospital. . .lots of friends. . .'

'I know, bless you, Ali. But that's not what I meant. . .' Maggie trailed off and looked out of the window again.

'You mean Ted?' Ali ventured at last.

Maggie nodded. 'I suppose I must do.'

'How long were you married?' she asked gently.

'Nine years.'

'It's a long time.'

'You become as one. . .' Maggie swallowed. 'It's hard to lose that. . . Sorry, Ali, it's difficult to explain.'

'You don't have to,' said Ali quietly. 'I know what you mean.'

Maggie raised her eyebrows slightly. 'Connor?' she said.

Ali nodded. Outside, the rain continued to hammer on the roof of the car. 'Yes,' she agreed at last, 'we were together for two years but it really was like being married. Trouble was when things went wrong we gave up. And that was as much my fault as Connor's. Maybe if we had been married we would have worked at it a bit harder.'

'It didn't work for us,' Maggie shrugged.

'It did for nine years,' protested Ali.

'True, but when the crunch came I couldn't cope with Ted's unfaithfulness. I really hated him then, Ali. I was so full of bitterness. So why is it now that the chips are down for me I find myself wondering whether I shouldn't have forgiven him and taken him back when he wanted me to?'

'Maybe none of us try hard enough at relationships, whether we are married or not,' said Ali.

With a deep sigh Maggie leaned forward and switched on the engine. 'You and Connor seemed to be getting on all right on Saturday night,' she said.

'That was a one-off,' replied Ali abruptly, 'believe me.'

'Really?' Maggie threw her a quick glance and drew out onto the main road. 'So you've no intention of trying to resurrect that particular relationship, then?'

'There's no point,' Ali replied. 'Too much has happened since.' As she spoke, a mental picture of Connor laughing with his petite, blonde companion flashed into her mind. Then, just as Maggie opened her mouth to say something else, she quickly changed the subject. Now was not the moment to tell Maggie what she had seen. Instead, she said, 'What about you and Ted?'

'What about me and Ted?'

'Will you tell him about this?'

'There's no point. He won't want to know.'

'But. . .'

'He has his own life now,' said Maggie firmly and Ali thought she detected a trace of bitterness in her tone and then, if she had been in any doubt, she added, 'and it doesn't include me.'

Ali bit her lip. She had been about to say that she felt sure that Ted would want to know; that he would care; that she had seen him on Saturday night watching Maggie when he had thought no one was looking, but something about Maggie's manner stopped her.

Because it was raining so hard she decided to leave her bicycle at the hospital and asked Maggie if she would take her right home.

'Come and have a bite to eat with me,' Ali added impulsively as Maggie drew up in Church Close. 'It's only salad and pizza but you are very welcome to share it with me.'

'No, thank you, Ali,' Maggie replied. 'You've been so kind but, if you don't mind, I think I'll get on home.'

'All right. If you're sure,' she said. Any other time she knew that Maggie would have jumped at the invitation. 'I'll see you tomorrow.' She paused, one hand on the door-catch of the car, and looked over her shoulder. 'Oh, Maggie?' she said.

'Yes?'

'Will you tell the others?'

Maggie shrugged. 'I don't see why not. Harvey will have to know as I'll need time off to see Tim Bartholomew. And, no doubt, the others will get to know in due course. Besides, I can't see any point in being secretive about these things.'

Ali got out of the car and bent down, looking inside again before she shut the door to say, 'Just as long as I know. I didn't want to go putting my foot in it. I'll see you tomorrow, then, Maggie.'

'Bye, Ali. Thanks for coming with me. I really appreciate it.'

She stood and watched for a moment, oblivious to the steadily falling rain, as Maggie drove out of the close. With a little sigh she turned to the house, only to be greeted by a reproachful Boy Blue who was highly indignant not only at being shut out in the rain but at being made to wait for his supper.

It had in many ways been a strange day but Ali found that the seriousness of Maggie's problem somehow helped her to keep her own problems in perspective.

For a while she had almost fancied that she might have wanted Connor back; would have been prepared to give their relationship another try. But, after talking to Maggie, she had been reminded of some of the more difficult aspects of the relationship they'd had and, if that had not been enough, seeing him with the woman he intended marrying had finally put paid to any lingering fantasies she might have been harbouring.

The following morning she walked to the hospital and by the time she entered A and E she was wary of seeing Connor, fearing that he might be under some misapprehension over their last meeting. She needn't have worried, however, as she found that other matters had taken precedence that morning.

Maggie had told both Harvey and Connor about her problem. Her GP had telephoned Tim Bartholomew the previous evening and because an appointment had been arranged for later that day Harvey was already trying to arrange cover.

'Did you know about this?' Connor asked Ali as Maggie hurried off to the staff-room to change into her uniform.

'Not until yesterday,' she replied. 'I persuaded her to go to her GP.'

'So how long had she known about it?'

'Only since Sunday.'

'Well, let's hope it's been caught in plenty of time,' said Connor. He paused and looked searchingly at Ali. 'Are you OK?' he said softly.

'Of course.' She stiffened. 'Why shouldn't I be?' She began to edge away. She too had to get changed and it seemed as good an excuse as any to curtail the direction she feared Connor's questioning was about to take.

'I just wondered, that's all.' He fell into step beside her as if he didn't intend giving up that easily. 'Good night Saturday, wasn't it?' The question was casual but she detected the edge behind it.

'Yes,' she replied coolly, equally as casual. 'Yes, it was. Pretty good as barbeques go.' She sensed rather than saw the glance her threw her but knew that it was faintly puzzled. No doubt her coolness surprised him.

'I thought it was just like old times,' he said softly as they reached the door to the nurses' room. 'I wondered if we could perhaps repeat the experience some time. . .'

She opened the door, stepped inside and, knowing that he could hardly follow her, looked back over her shoulder. 'No, Connor,' she said firmly, 'it wasn't like old times. It wasn't like old times at all, and we quite definitely won't be repeating the experience.'

'But, Ali, there's something I want to explain. . .'

Fleetingly aware of the surprise in his blue eyes, she shut the door in his face.

Maybe that would put paid to his games, she thought as briefly she leaned against the closed door. Quite obviously he had thought he was onto a good thing. She'd been prepared on Saturday to give him the benefit of the doubt; that maybe for them both it really had been just a trip down memory lane, but now she wondered.

The look in his eyes this morning suggested that he wanted more. She'd seen that look before and she knew exactly what it meant. He probably thought that a bit of two-timing wouldn't do any harm—that his girlfriend would never know if he had one last fling. Well, if that was his game he could forget it, at least with her, Ali thought angrily, because she quite definitely didn't want to play.

For one moment, on Saturday night, she had been shocked as the intensity of her feelings had almost got the better of her.

Now, she quite definitely had those feelings firmly under control again. Now, she was just so relieved that she hadn't given in to those feelings; hadn't let them get the better of her and make it obvious that she had wanted Connor to make love her her again.

And now the roles had apparently been reversed and it was Connor, not her, who wanted to take the matter further. Ali knew from past experience that great care would be needed in all her future dealings with Connor so that anything she did could not be misconstrued as giving him encouragement.

When she got back to the nurses' station she had no time for further speculation about Connor's intentions as the waiting area was rapidly filling up and an ambulance had just arrived.

'Would you and Jessica take this one, please, Ali?' said Harvey as the paramedics carried an elderly man into the treatment room.

'What can you tell us, Mac?' asked Ali as she and Jessica followed the paramedics.

'Its old Monty Pascoe again,' said Mac. 'He's been knocked down by a car. Looks like he spent the night under the viaduct, then wandered out this morning into the rush hour to cross the road.'

'Has he been in before?' whispered Jessica as the two paramedics, together with Harvey and Joe, lifted the patient onto the bed.

'Many times,' replied Ali. 'He used to live in Denehurst and then he moved away—to Southampton, we think. But he's been back in this area for some time now. As you can smell from his breath, he has been drinking.'

'That's not the only smell!' murmured Jessica.

'You're right. I'm afraid Monty has neglected his hygiene and general appearance for a long time now.' Ali approached the bed and looked down at the patient. 'Hello, Monty,' she said, noticing that his coat and trousers were ragged, wet, and covered in mud.

'He's grazed his head,' said Mac, 'but we couldn't establish any other injury. When we arrived he was sitting on the kerb. Anyway, he's all yours now. We'll leave you to it. See you, Monty.' The paramedics moved away.

'Thanks, boys.' Ali glanced up and was just in time to see Joe wink at Jessica as he too left the treatment room. She threw the student a quick look and was amused to see that she was blushing. Turning back to the patient, she said, 'Can you tell me what happened, Monty?'

'I don't really remember.' Monty's voice was quiet and cultured and Ali noticed that Jessica looked up in surprise, forgetting her confusion of only seconds earlier. 'One moment I was preparing to cross the road,' Monty went on, 'and the next I was sitting talking to those kind gentlemen of yours who told me they were going to take me to St Mark's.'

'Well, first, Monty, we will take your temperature, your pulse and blood pressure,' said Ali. 'Then we'll get the doctor to examine you. After that, we'll see about getting you cleaned up. You've got mud all over you,' she added tactfully.

'It gets very damp on that river bank,' Monty said seriously.

'I can imagine,' said Ali. 'Now, is there anyone we can inform that you are here?'

Monty shook his head. 'No,' he said. 'No one.'

'And do you have an address in Denehurst?'

'I used to,' he replied. 'I used to live in Pelhurst Avenue.'

'And now, Monty?' asked Ali gently.

'No,' he sighed and a far-away look came into his watery blue eyes, 'not now.'

'Well, never mind.' Ali glanced up as she finished taking his blood pressure. 'Here's Dr Stevens now,' she said as Connor came into the treatment room.

'Hello,' he said. 'Mr Pascoe, I believe.'

'Yes, sir,' said Monty.

'I understand you've had a disagreement with a car,' said Connor. 'Any injuries, Nurse?' He turned to Ali.

'Only the graze to his head, Doctor,' she replied. 'Temperature, pulse and blood pressure are all normal.'

'Good, well, let's have a look at you, then, Mr Pascoe,' said Connor.

The only injuries to be found were a slight bruising to the pelvis and the graze on Monty's forehead.

'I think,' said Connor as he concluded his examination, 'a bath next and then I dare say a cup of tea and
perhaps some toast wouldn't come amiss.'

While Monty was in the bath his case was discussed
by the rest of the team.

'His injuries don't justify admission to an accident
bed,' said Harvey, 'and he's neither dehydrated nor
hypothermic.'

'Is he an alcoholic?' asked Jessica.

'Let's say he is probably becoming increasingly
dependent on cheap alcohol,' said Connor. 'And he is
quite obviously homeless.'

'A case for Social Services, I think,' said Harvey.
'I'll give Welfare a ring and they can make some
arrangements.'

'I don't understand it,' said Jessica. 'How has he
become like this? He said he had a house once in
Denehurst and he speaks. . .well, I was really surprised
when I heard him speak. . .'

'Monty Pascoe is a highly educated man,' said
Harvey. 'He seemed to go to pieces after his wife died.
He couldn't come to terms with her death. He started
walking the streets some time ago, I believe. He's been
brought in here on numerous occasions.'

'But what happened to his house?' Jessica was quite
obviously still appalled that this could happen and to
such a person as Monty Pascoe.

'I don't know for sure,' replied Harvey. 'At a guess
I would say it fell into disrepair through neglect and I
wouldn't be surprised if vandals or even squatters
haven't got in by now.'

'But that's terrible.' Jessica was clearly upset. 'What
will happen to him? He's an old man, for goodness'
sake. We can't just send him back to sleep under the
viaduct!'

'I'm sure Social Services will offer some help,' said

Ali. 'Maybe a place in a residential home for the
elderly.'

'But whether that is what Monty wants remains to
be seen,' said Connor.

'Surely it would be for his own good?' retorted
Jessica.

'Maybe.' Connor stood up. 'But the fact remains you
can't force people to do something they don't want to
do, even if it is for their own good.'

Jessica still seemed agitated, even after the hospital
welfare officer arrived and Monty was put into her care.

Later, as they took a coffee-break, to try to distract
the girl Ali brought the conversation round to Joe.

'He's a nice lad,' she said casually, handing Jessica
a mug of coffee, and when the girl only nodded in reply
she went on, 'You and he seemed to get on well at the
barbeque.'

'Yes, we did.' Jessica took the mug and curled her
hands around it as if she was cold. 'He's asked me out,'
she said abruptly but before Ali could say any more
she said, 'He reminded me of my grandad, you know.'

'Who, Joe?' Ali looked up sharply from the coffee-
machine.

'No.' Jessica sighed and shook her head. 'No, not
Joe. Monty—Monty Pascoe. He was so like him. He
spoke like him. He even looked a bit like him under
all that dirt and matted hair. At one point when I was
helping him to undress for his bath, I even found myself
thinking he was my grandad.'

'I think Monty would have liked that,' said Ali.

'What?' Jessica frowned and when she realised what
Ali had said she gave a slight shrug. 'Maybe,' she said,
then went on, 'but all I can think is how awful it would
have been if that had been my grandad. . . If my gran
had died and he couldn't cope. . . He would hate to be

like that. . .I just know he would. . . He's a very proud man, you see. . .'

'As I'm sure Monty was once,' said Ali quietly. 'Still is, probably. . .'

'I know.' Jessica stared into her mug for a long moment and, looking up at Ali, said, 'It's awful, isn't it?'

'What is, the way we fail people?' asked Ali quietly and when Jessica nodded she said, 'Yes, it is awful, but what Connor said was true as well—that sometimes, no matter how much we want to help people they simply don't want to be helped. . . Now, getting back to young Joe,' she added after a while, 'you say he's asked you out?'

Jessica nodded. 'Yes, he's really nice, you know. It's funny but he is the exact opposite to Dave—not usually the type I go for at all. I can't believe how well we got on.' She fell silent for a moment, reflecting, then quietly she said, 'I'm so glad you told me not to move in with Dave unless I was sure I was really ready for that. I wasn't ready, Ali. I really wasn't.'

'I think you were aware of that without me having to tell you,' said Ali, sipping her own coffee.

'Maybe.' Jessica shrugged. 'But having you say it as well. . .' She trailed off and after a moment added, 'I thought, you see, that living with him would solve all those doubts, when in actual fact they would probably only have made them worse. . . Then, when I said no and he wanted to cool things, I thought it was the end of the world—I really did. I thought I had made a terrible mistake and that in not moving in with him when he wanted I had missed my chance, that I would never have another chance like it. . .'

'And then you met Joe,' smiled Ali.

'Yes,' agreed Jessica, 'and then I met Joe. And I'm

so happy. Honestly, Ali, I didn't know I could be so happy.'

'Which is exactly the way it should be at your age,' said Ali quickly realising that she had just been hit by a sudden stab of envy.

'What about you?' asked Jessica suddenly.

'Me?' Ali feigned surprise, but she had a feeling what was coming next and mentally braced herself.

'Yes,' Jessica swept on, 'you and Dr Stevens seemed to be getting on very well at the barbeque.'

'We had a good time, yes,' admitted Ali casually, 'but that's as far as it goes.'

'Oh!' Jessica looked disappointed. 'I thought. . .'

'You thought what, Jessica?' Ali raised her eyebrows.

'I thought. . . Well, Maggie said. . .' Jessica flushed and trailed off.

'Maggie said what?' asked Ali coolly.

'Well. . .' Jessica looked uncomfortable and squirmed on her chair. 'I had the feeling that it might have been Dr Stevens that you lived with once. . .you told me, remember, that there had been someone—? Well, I asked Maggie and she said that, yes, it was him but that I was to keep quiet about it. . .so I did. But, then, seeing you. . .seeing you both at the barbeque, you looked so perfect together. . .and I just wondered. . .'

'Well, you can forget it,' said Ali crisply. 'Dr Stevens has other commitments.'

'Oh, I hoped. . .' Jessica looked so disappointed that Ali gave a short laugh and, then draining her mug, she stood up.

'Just let it be a further warning to you,' she added. 'Another case of living with someone not necessarily being the answer. . . Dr Stevens quite obviously proved to himself that I wasn't the woman for him. . .so he's now found the one who is. Come on—' she glanced at the clock '—it's time we were back on duty.'

Without another word Jessica joined her and together they left the staff-room and were on their way back to the nurses' station when they met Maggie.

'Going for your break?' asked Ali and as Maggie shook her head she said, 'You go on, Jessica. I'll be with you in a moment.' As the girl went on into Reception, she turned questioningly back to Maggie.

'I'm just going to freshen up,' said Maggie, 'then I'm off up to see Tim Bartholomew. Wish me luck, Ali.'

'Oh, Maggie, I do. Of course I do.' Impulsively Ali leaned forward and kissed Maggie on the cheek. 'You'll be fine,' she said. 'I just know you will.'

'Thanks,' Maggie whispered, unable to say another word, and with eyes suddenly suspiciously bright she put her head down and hurried down the corridor to the staff-room.

Ali watched her until the staff-room door closed behind her then, swallowing deeply, she too turned and hurried in the opposite direction back to the hustle and bustle of A and E.

CHAPTER ELEVEN

MAGGIE was admitted to hospital the next afternoon, surgery for the excision of her breast lump scheduled for the following morning.

As the early shift on A and E drew to a close Ali announced her intention of going up to see Maggie before she went home.

'Give her our love,' said Beth.

'Yes, and tell her we are all thinking about her,' added Harvey.

'Of course.' Ali slipped out of the staff-room, only to find Connor at her side.

'Mind if I join you?' he said.

Ali hesitated. She did mind, if she was honest. She wanted to see Maggie on her own but, quite apart from that, she had already made up her mind that she wanted as little to do with Connor as possible in future, especially out of working hours. Going visiting with him, even if it was to see a mutual friend, didn't exactly fit in with this new regime. It would, however, seem petty to refuse under the circumstances so she found herself murmuring that, no, of course she didn't mind.

They found Maggie sitting in an easy chair in a small, four-bedded ward. She looked white and strained but she seemed pleased to see them.

'Come to see the condemned prisoner?' she joked bravely.

'Where?' Connor made a show of looking round. 'I don't see one.'

Ali drew up a chair and Connor leaned against a

radiator. 'Is there anything you want?' Ali glanced at Maggie's locker, which was empty apart from a jug of water and a tumbler.

Maggie shook her head. 'I don't intend being here longer than I can help,' she said, pulling a face. 'It's perfectly true, you know, what they say about us nurses making dreadful patients. Honestly, Ali, I hate it—and I've only been here a couple of hours. I shall certainly try and be a bit more sympathetic with my patients when I get back to work. . .that is. . .if. . .'

'Has Tim Bartholomew been down to see you?' Connor interrupted.

'Yes,' Maggie nodded. 'And Miles Hedges, the anaesthetist. Tim said I had to be positive. . .'

'Absolutely. . .' said Connor.

'And he said he was very optimistic. . .'

'Well, there you are. . .' said Ali.

'But he had to say that, didn't he?' said Maggie. When neither Ali nor Connor answered, she said, 'Come on, we all know this could go either way. It could be a harmless, benign little lump that when it is removed will give no more trouble, or it could be a little monster that will require not only possibly radical surgery but radiation and months of chemotherapy. . .' She trailed off and glanced sharply at Ali. 'Listen,' she added, as Ali sought desperately for something reassuring to say, 'there is something you can do for me.'

'Yes?' said Ali eagerly. At that moment she was prepared to move heaven and earth for Maggie if it would make her feel better.

'I've been thinking,' said Maggie, 'about something you said the other day, Ali, and I've decided that I would like Ted to know about this. If things don't go very well tomorrow, well, I wouldn't like him to hear from anyone else. You see, I know how I would feel if it was the other way round. . .if Ted was in hospital and I didn't know. . .so I wondered, do you think if I gave you his address you could go and tell him?'

'Of course I will,' said Ali.

'I suppose I could phone,' Maggie hesitated, 'but it may come as a bit of a shock with me actually being in hospital. After all, Ted only saw me last Saturday at the barbeque.'

'There's no problem, Maggie,' said Ali. 'I'll go this evening.'

Maggie reached for her handbag, took out a notebook and pen and scribbled on a blank page. 'The only thing is,' she said, tearing off the page and handing it to Ali, 'he lives on the other side of Denehurst, and with you not having a car. . .'

'Don't worry about that.' Connor leaned forward and read the piece of paper over Ali's shoulder. 'I know where that is. I'll take Ali over there.'

Ali swallowed. She wanted to protest; wanted to say that she didn't want him to take her but she didn't want to make a fuss, especially at such a time, so she kept silent.

She was just wondering whether she could get Connor to go on his own when Maggie leaned her head back and briefly closed her eyes.

'Thanks, Ali,' she said. 'Ted knows about you and what good friends we are. I was able to point you out to him on Saturday so it won't be like a complete stranger arriving to give him bad news.'

They left Maggie shortly after that and took the lift to the ground floor. As the doors closed, Connor said, 'Do you want to go home first and have me pick you up later. . .?'

'No,' she said quickly. That was the last thing she wanted; that would make it seem like a date. 'No, I think I'd like to go now.'

'Very well,' he shrugged. 'Just as you like.'

For the second time that week she left her bicycle at the hospital but this time it was Connor's car she got into, wondering as she did so what on earth they were going to talk about.

'It sounds,' he said as he drew out of the hospital car park, 'as if Maggie and Ted still care a lot about each other, in spite of their divorce.'

'It would seem that way.' Ali agreed.

'I think some groups of the animal kingdom have got it right,' said Connor after a moment.

'What do you mean?' She threw him a startled glance.

'Well, they've never heard of divorce. When they take a mate it's for life and I'm not sure if, basically, it isn't like that for humans as well. We try to be sophisticated and pretend these things don't matter but biologically maybe they do...maybe those ties with one's mate are forged for life.'

Ali didn't answer. Suddenly she felt as if the conversation was heading for dangerous waters.

They drove in silence for a time after that, through the centre of Denehurst and into the more highly populated residential area. It was a warm summer's evening with glimpses of blue sky visible through the thick foliage of the trees that lined the roads. When Ali opened the car window the heavy scent of roses hung in the air.

Ted Hoskins lived in the basement of a large house divided into flats. When Ali rang the doorbell, to her dismay there was no reply. She rang it again, only too aware of Connor watching her from the car.

'There's no one in.' A woman with straggly hair and wearing a hippy-style skirt which reached her ankles suddenly appeared at the top of the basement steps.

'Have you any idea what time Mr Hoskins gets in?' asked Ali.

'About an hour's time,' said the woman, shrugging thin shoulders.

'Oh, I see. Thank you.' Slowly Ali made her way back to the car.

'Isn't he there?' asked Connor.

Ali shook her head. 'According to that lady, who I would say was a neighbour, he won't be home for another hour. . .'

'So we've got some time to kill,' said Connor as she got back into the car.

'I suppose I could come back later this evening,' she began.

'Only to find Ted's gone out again. . . It's a fair old distance by bike, you know.'

'Yes, I suppose it is.'

'Tell you what,' said Connor. 'I know what we'll do. There's something I'd like you to see.' He glanced at his watch. 'Should take about an hour or so. . .'

'What is it?' she said quickly.

'You'll see.' He switched on the engine.

Ali bit her lip. She didn't want to go anywhere with him but she really didn't know quite what else to suggest, having promised Maggie that she would see that Ted got the message that evening.

She remained silent as Connor drove, and her curiosity grew as they left the residential, tree-lined avenues behind and drove out of Denehurst into the lush green of the countryside.

It wasn't until they left the main road and entered a network of narrow country lanes that the first germ of suspicion stirred in her mind. But surely, she thought, dismissing the thought even as it formed, Connor wouldn't do that. He wouldn't take her to the farm cottage he was preparing for the woman he was planning to marry. He couldn't be that cruel, that insensitive.

She threw him a half-fearful glance but he was staring straight ahead, concentrating on the twists and turns of the lanes. It was only when he finally pulled off the

lane and the car began bumping down a track and Ali
caught sight of a painted sign, partly obscured by over-
hanging hawthorn, that her worst fears were realised
and she knew that they were indeed heading for
Langstone Farm.

They drove through a flurry of chickens and passed
the main buildings; the stone farmhouse, cowsheds, out-
houses and a large barn. To the frantic barking of a
Border collie, Connor brought the car to a halt before
a small terrace of farm labourers' cottages.

'I can't imagine why you have brought me here,'
said Ali in a tight little voice as he switched off the
engine.

'I thought you might be interested.' He sounded
genuinely surprised. 'After all, this is going to be
my home.'

Ali didn't answer. She could barely trust herself to
speak as her anger threatened to get the better of her.

'Come and have a look.' Connor got out of the car
and, when she made no attempt to move, he came round
to her side of the car and opened the door. 'There is
still a lot of work to be done. I've had a local builder,
Tom Simmonds, in to do the structural work. He's a
great guy is Tom, but he's almost finished and the rest
is going to be down to me.'

'You amaze me,' replied Ali coldly. She didn't want
to know about the building work; didn't want to know
what a great guy Tom Simmonds was, and she certainly
didn't want to know about Connor's sudden interest in
home improvements.

As if he sensed her disinterest, Connor said, 'Come
and have a look at the view, then. That is something
that will interest you.'

Slowly she got out of the car. She really didn't think
that she could go on sitting there and ignoring him or
the situation. He might think that she was sulking and

that was the last thing she wanted. Determinedly she
strode up to the front door of the cottage and then had
to wait as, with a maddening smile, he followed her,
produced a key from his pocket and unlocked the door.

She had been hoping that it would be awful, with
everything in the worst possible taste, but of course it
wasn't. Two cottages had been knocked into one and
the rooms on the ground floor all opened into each
other. The stone walls had been whitewashed, the low
ceilings were supported by the original oak beams and
the floors were flagstoned and uneven. Window-frames
had been replaced but the new blended cleverly with
the old, as did the carefully restored stone fireplace.

With a sinking heart Ali stood in the middle of the
empty rooms and looked round.

Connor was going to live here. Live here with that
woman, the petite blonde she had seen with him in
his car.

'Do you like it?' he asked, leaning against the
window-sill and watching her.

'Yes,' she said, desperately trying to sound casual.
'Yes, it's. . .very nice,' she added ineffectually.

Connor continued to watch her then, pushing himself
away from the window-sill, he said, 'Come and have a
look upstairs.'

She was about to refuse. She didn't want to see the
bedrooms, didn't want to be able to picture what would
happen there.

'That's where you will see the view,' he said.

Meekly she followed him. After all, she didn't want
him to think it would disturb her in any way, seeing
the room where he and his wife would. . .

'Mind your head,' he said as they climbed a narrow
staircase. 'The beams are very low. I've bashed my head
several times already—it teaches you to remember.'

The bedrooms were just what she had imagined.

Pretty little rooms tucked away under the eaves with casement windows which, when opened, revealed the view, a view so glorious that for one moment Ali forgot the pain behind what she was seeing.

Pastures with grazing cattle rolled gently away immediately below the cottage windows, then opened out into a lush green valley. In the distance, beyond the water meadows, the river meandered like a lazy silver snake and a distant church spire gleamed in the late sunshine.

'Oh, it's beautiful,' she gasped, and as Connor opened the window she leaned out, taking in deep lungfuls of the soft summer air thick with the sweet scent of the honeysuckle that climbed the cottage walls.

'I thought you might like it,' he said quietly.

Gradually, as she stood there, she became very, very aware of his presence, of his closeness to her. The familiarity of him, the male scent. Why, if she turned, she could almost be in his arms. . .

'Tell me,' she said quickly after a moment, craning her neck slightly, 'that spire, is it the church in the close. . .?'

'The very same,' he murmured. 'So, in theory, I could lie in bed here, look out of the window and see where you are.'

She frowned. She wasn't sure she liked the idea of that. She would be alone while he, Connor, would be lying here in a bed in this very room, possibly having just made love. She dismissed the thought before it could get out of control and consume her in a wave of blind jealousy, and turned abruptly away from the window.

'Ali,' Connor murmured and, reaching out his hand, his fingers brushed her shoulder, burning like fire through the thin fabric of her cotton shirt.

She froze, unable to move—gripped suddenly by an

intolerable, overwhelming longing for him to take her
in his arms again and love her in the way he had done
so often in the past.

'Ali,' he said softly, his voice suddenly husky as if
he too was overwhelmed by the intensity of the moment,
'about the other evening. . .I'm sorry. . .I should not
have. . .'

'It's all right,' she said sharply. 'It wasn't just you. . .
it was as much me. . .'

He sighed but didn't move so that she remained
trapped between him and the window. 'It's just,' he
said after a moment, 'that it's so hard to act as if nothing
ever happened between us, when so much did.'

'I know. . .' she whispered, not daring to look up into
his face, afraid of what she might see in his eyes and
afraid that this time all self-control would vanish for
them both.

'I was a fool, letting you go, Ali,' he said at last.
'You were the best thing that ever happened to me.'

She remained very still, listening but hardly able to
believe what she was hearing.

'My only excuse is that I was very young,
headstrong. . .'

'Wild, Connor,' she said tightly. 'You were wild. . .'

'Yes, wild,' he admitted. 'But you, you were so good
for me. You taught me how to love, Ali.'

She did look at him then, raising her eyebrows in
almost sceptical surprise so that he laughed. 'Oh, I don't
mean how to make love. . . I mean how to love. What
it means to care about someone else; to care about them
more than you care about yourself. . . The trouble was
that I didn't see it until after you'd gone. By then it
was too late. . . But I'll always be grateful to you, Ali.
You taught me so much about myself. . .'

She continued staring at him, amazed by what she
was hearing, and then, as the truth and the tragedy of

what he was saying finally dawned on her, she lowered her head and with a muttered exclamation she pushed past him, crossed the room and clattered down the stairs, only just remembering to lower her head beneath the beams.

Maybe what he had said was true. Maybe she had taught him a lot about himself; tamed his wild ways; taught him how to love. . . The trouble was that it would not be she who would reap the benefit—it would be the woman with whom he was to share this cottage.

Without a backward glance, she hurried out of the cottage and tugged open the car door. By the time Connor came out and had locked the front door she was sitting in the car with the door shut.

He got into the car and shut his own door but made no attempt to start the engine. Instead he said, 'Ali, I think we need to talk.'

'I don't see we have anything to talk about,' she replied crisply.

'Yes,' he said, 'we do. . .'

'No, Connor, we don't. What happened between you and me is in the past. It's over and we both have to get on with our lives. Now—' she glanced at her watch '—can we go? Ted should be home by now. We don't want to get back there and find he's gone out again.'

For a moment she thought Connor was going to argue but, without a word, he switched on the engine. As they drew away from the cottages she kept her eyes straight, not wanting even one more glance at the paradise that was to be Connor's home.

They were silent on the drive back to Ted Hoskin's house. It was not a comfortable silence and all that Ali wanted was to see Ted, deliver the message and go home. She was just wondering what she would do if Ted still hadn't arrived home when Connor stopped the car outside the house and she saw to her relief that a large motorbike was parked on the path that led to the basement.

Ted answered the door immediately, almost as if he had been waiting for her and had watched her from behind the net-curtained window as she came down the basement steps.

'Hello,' he said, eyeing her speculatively, 'you're Ali, aren't you?'

'That's right,' she nodded and in turn summed up his appearance. He was short for a man, and thick set. He wore jeans and a rather grubby T-shirt open at the front to reveal a very hairy chest. His greying fair hair was thinning on top and for one moment Ali found herself wondering what it was that bound Maggie to this man.

Then he smiled, the magic word 'charisma' entered her mind and she knew. 'I saw you the other night,' he said. 'Maggie has told me all about you.'

'She has?' For a moment she was thrown off guard. Something in the expression in his eyes suggested that he knew rather more about her than he should.

He nodded and when it seemed he was about to say more Ali quickly intervened, 'Actually, it's about Maggie that I've come.'

She watched his expression change as she explained what was happening, and if she had been in any doubt before as to this man's feelings for his ex-wife by the end she was in no doubt at all. She saw surprise change to concern and then to raw, naked fear.

'I think she would like to see you tonight, Ted,' she said. 'If you go soon you shouldn't have any difficulty getting in—visiting may be over but I'm sure, under the circumstances, they will let you in.'

'Let them try stopping me,' he said. 'I'll go now.' Pausing only to grab his jacket from a hook behind the door, he joined Ali in the small yard. 'How did you get here?' he asked. 'Can I give you a lift?' He nodded towards the motorbike.

'No, thanks.' She glanced back at him as he followed her up the basement steps. 'I already have a lift.' As they reached the pavement she glanced towards Connor sitting in the car.

'Oh, I see.' Ted looked surprised, then he said, 'Well, thanks for coming. I'm much obliged to you. Thanks, mate.' He nodded towards Connor but as he turned to his motorbike he paused and said, 'I see it worked, then. I bet Maggie was pleased.'

'Sorry?' Ali frowned.

'You two.' He nodded towards Connor again. 'Maggie said she thought it looked as if it was working on Saturday night... Anyway, I must get going...but just one thing...' He hesitated. 'Maggie,' he said at last, 'she will be all right, won't she?' The fear was back in his eyes.

'I'm sure she will, Ted,' said Ali as reassuringly as she could, 'just as I'm sure that seeing you will make her feel a whole lot better...just to know that someone cares...'

'She need have no fears on that score.' Ted rocked his motorbike forward off its stand and Ali walked round to the passenger side of the car and opened the door.

'Mission accomplished?' asked Connor as she got in and fastened her seat belt.

'Yes,' she nodded and they both sat for a moment and watched as Ted wheeled his motorbike onto the road, secured his crash helmet and finally, with a wave of his hand, roared away.

Even when Ted was out of sight Connor made no attempt to start the car, almost as if he was waiting for her to say something.

She didn't, however, choosing to remain silent even

after Connor at last started the car—trying to make sense on her own of what Ted had said. She knew that Connor had heard and instinctively knew that he had understood; that there had been something going on of which she had been unaware, but she wanted to try and reason it out for herself before she asked him.

Ted had been almost pleased when he had seen that it was Connor who had given her a lift and had gone on to imply that he was glad that something had worked—that Maggie would be pleased it had worked.

But that what had worked? Whatever it was had something to do with Saturday night. Something that Maggie had thought was working then.

She threw Connor a sidelong glance but his expression was inscrutable as he concentrated on his driving.

They only spoke once on the drive home and it was Connor who broke the silence. 'How did he take it?' he asked and Ali knew that he was referring to Ted.

'He was shocked, of course,' she said, then added, 'and he cares, whatever Maggie may think. He really does care. Wild horses wouldn't have kept him away from that hospital tonight.'

They fell silent again until they drew up outside the little house in Church Close. By that time Ali had given up trying to work out what Ted had meant. It simply didn't make any sense.

'What did he mean?' she said at last, making no attempt to get out of the car.

'Who?' asked Connor innocently.

'You know who. Ted, back there,' she said sharply. 'What did he mean when he said it had worked?'

'You tell me,' replied Connor in the same innocent tone.

'No, Connor,' she retorted, 'you tell me. Because I

didn't have a clue what he was talking about, while you. . .'

'You think I knew?' he asked.

'I damn well know you knew. I know you too well, Connor.'

'Ah, yes,' he said. 'You do, don't you, Ali? Silly of me to think I could hide anything from you.'

'Oh,' she said quickly, 'so you admit there is something being hidden from me. Something I don't know about!'

'I'm not admitting anything.'

She stared at him in exasperation. 'What did Ted mean about Saturday night?' she demanded. 'What about Saturday night?'

'I suppose he was referring to the barbeque,' said Connor.

'Yes, I supposed he was as well,' she replied impatiently, 'but he said something about Maggie being pleased about something working. . . What the hell did he mean, Connor?'

'Goodness knows,' he shrugged. 'Maybe Maggie was simply pleased that we seemed to be getting on so well together again. I get the impression she's a bit of a match-maker.'

'But why would she have been pleased?' she demanded. 'Maggie knows the score. She knows you are practically married to someone else. Why, it was Maggie in the first place who told me about your cottage and about all the work you've been doing there. . .'

'Yes.' He didn't seem surprised, 'I did tell Maggie. . .'

'So why would she be pleased, or even think that. . .? Why, she even knew I didn't want to work with you and didn't want to be where you were. . .so why would she. . .?'

'Be pleased at the prospect of you and I getting

back together again?' He raised his eyebrows.

'Yes. . .'

'Do you think it might have had anything to do with the fact that I told her that was what I wanted?' he asked softly.

She stared at him, thinking just for one moment that he had gone mad. 'But how can it be what you want?' she demanded at last. 'What about this woman? This other woman, the one you came to Denehurst to be near?'

Connor in turn stared at her, his gaze roaming over her face, her hair and finally coming to rest on her mouth.

'There is no other woman, Ali,' he said quietly at last. 'There never was. There was only you. I came to Denehurst to be close to you.'

CHAPTER TWELVE

ALI stared at Connor, unable to take in what he was saying. 'What do you mean,' she said at last, ' "There is no other woman"?'

'What I say,' he replied quietly, calmly. 'There is no other woman,' he repeated.

'There is!' she said. 'Of course there is. I saw her.'

'Saw her?' Connor frowned.

'Yes. With you, in this car.'

The frown on his face deepened. 'I don't understand—you couldn't have seen her, Ali—she doesn't exist.' Suddenly a small smile played around his mouth as if he found something amusing.

'So you're trying to tell me I was hallucinating,' said Ali. 'For God's sake, Connor, I might have been guillable once, but not now! I know what I saw!'

'Ali, please calm down!'

'I am calm!' she retorted.

'Well, I'm sorry,' said Connor, 'but I'm afraid you are going to have to refresh my memory because I haven't got a clue what you are talking about.'

She stared at him in exasperation, but to her amazement she saw that his puzzlement really did seem genuine.

'So are you saying you're having problems with your memory as well?' She raised her eyebrows, trying hard to remain cool. She was only too used to Connor's gift for talking himself out of tight situations—too often in the past he had sweet-talked her round.

'As far as I know there is nothing wrong with my memory,' he said.

'Well, we are only talking about Monday evening, for heaven's sake!'

'Monday evening. . .?'

'Yes, I suppose you're going to say I dreamt seeing you in Denehurst High Street, when you stopped your car outside the hairdresser's and picked up. . .picked up your. . .your passenger!'

'My passenger. . .?' Suddenly his expression cleared. 'Oh, you mean Lucy?' He laughed and Ali felt a sharp stab of pain. She knew her name now. She didn't want to know her name. 'But where were you?' he added in sudden surprise.

'I had just come out of the supermarket,' she replied icily. 'I was waiting to cross the road.'

'I didn't see you. . .'

'No, you wouldn't have done. You were far more concerned with what you were doing. . .'

'Well, it was raining. . .'

'I know it was raining. . .'

'Lucy had just had her hair done. . .'

'Oh, bully for Lucy! I got wet.'

'I'm sorry, Ali. I really am.' For one moment Connor looked as if he was struggling not to laugh. 'I simply didn't see you. You see, I wasn't sure exactly where the hairdresser's was. I knew it was on that side of the High Street—near Woolworths, Tom had said.'

'Tom?' she said sharply. 'Who's Tom?' She didn't really want to know. She just felt irritated and exasperated with Connor.

'Tom is Lucy's husband,' said Connor quietly.

As he spoke the church clock began to chime the hour and Ali thought she had misheard him. 'What?' she said. 'What did you say?'

'I said,' Connor repeated quietly as the chimes ceased and the echo died away, 'that Tom Simmonds is Lucy's husband.'

Ali stared at him. She'd heard that name before—very recently.

'Tom is the builder who is working on the cottage,' Connor said.

Ali continued to stare at him in growing bewilderment.

'Monday was my day off,' Connor went on. 'I had been at the cottage all day, working with Tom. He had almost finished the fireplace but he had arranged to pick his wife up from the hairdresser's. I offered to go for him so that he could finish the job before the cement dried.'

'But. . .' She stared at him in shocked amazement. 'I thought. . .I thought. . .'

'I think I can guess what you thought,' he said quietly. Taking a deep breath, he said, 'Ali, I said earlier that I felt we needed to talk. You said then that there was nothing to talk about. Maybe now you have changed your mind?'

'I don't know. . .' Numbly she shook her head. 'I really don't know, Connor.' Her mind was in chaos.

'Could I come inside for a little while?' He nodded towards the house. 'There are things I think I need to explain.'

'You can say that again,' she said weakly.

'So, can we go inside?'

'I suppose so.' As if in a dream, she got out of the car and walked up to her front door but before slipping her key in the lock she absent-mindedly bent down to stroke Boy Blue, who had run to meet them. In the same dream-like state she picked up the post from the mat, then went through to the kitchen where she dumped her bag onto the worktop before automatically opening the cupboard and taking out a tin of cat food.

While she opened the tin and spooned the meat into Boy Blue's dish, her mind was still in turmoil.

The woman, the blonde, hadn't been his girlfriend after all.

There had been no other woman.

But if that was the case, why had he said there was—why had he lied?

She turned with Boy Blue's dish to find that Connor had picked up the cat and was stroking his head and ears while Boy Blue himself, possibly for the first time in his life, seemed more concerned with the attention he was receiving than with the prospect of his supper.

With a laugh Connor set the cat down on the floor and they both watched as at last Boy Blue, realising that there were other things to be considered, sniffed suspiciously at the contents of his bowl and then began to eat.

'Are you telling me, Connor,' said Ali, without looking at him, 'that you lied about there being another woman?'

'Let's say I invented the idea,' he replied.

'You lied.'

'Lied is a strong word, Ali.'

'All right. So you invented the idea. Why should you want to do that?'

He sighed. 'I was getting a little bit desperate.'

'I don't understand.'

He stared thoughtfully at her. 'If I remember rightly, you were threatening to leave. Isn't that so?'

'Yes,' she nodded. 'That's absolutely true. But I don't see why you should have thought that inventing another woman would have changed anything. . .'

'You don't?' He raised his eyebrows.

'No. . .'

'But it worked,' he said softly, 'didn't it?'

'I. . .I don't know what you mean.' She stared at him.

'Well, you didn't go, did you? You are still here.'

'That's true,' she frowned, 'but I. . .'

'So why didn't you go?' he said softly.

Suddenly she was lost for words. She could hardly say that she had stayed because she hadn't wanted him to think she couldn't bear the thought of seeing him with another woman.

'I took a gamble,' he said after a moment. 'I gambled that you wouldn't want me to think you still felt anything for me.'

She stared at him.

It worked, didn't it?' he said. 'The gamble paid off.'

'I. . .'

'It paid off, because you stayed.'

She turned away. 'So why did you come to Denehurst in the first place?' she said after a moment.

'I told you why,' he replied.

'You said it was to be near the woman you wanted to marry. . .' When he didn't reply she looked up sharply. 'Connor—' she took a deep breath '—did you know I was living in Denehurst?'

He nodded.

'And did you know I was working at St Mark's?'

When he nodded again she said, 'But you said it was a coincidence.'

'No.' He shook his head. 'You simply came to that conclusion.'

'So why?' she said helplessly. 'Why? Why come here. . .to Denehurst. . .to St Mark's which—let's face it, nice as it is—isn't exactly the greatest career move you could have made. . . And the cottage. . .why that, Connor?'

'It's a long story, Ali,' He looked helplessly at her. 'I don't really know where to start.'

'Maybe the beginning would be a good place,' she replied. Slowly she led the way out of the kitchen and into the sitting-room where, carefully ignoring the sofa, she indicated for Connor to sit in the rocking-chair while she chose a chair well away from him on the opposite side of the room.

For a while they sat in silence with Connor looking, if anything, a little shame-faced.

'Well, go on,' said Ali eventually, 'I'm listening.'

At that moment the door opened a fraction and Boy Blue nudged his way into the room. With his tail in the air, he ran straight across to Connor and, miaowing in delight, jumped onto his lap and settled down, purring happily.

'At least someone is pleased at my presence in Denehurst,' said Connor with a rueful grin then, seeing Ali's expression, he said hurriedly, 'OK. . explanations. . .'

He paused for a long moment as if considering, then he said, 'You know something, Ali? I was devastated when we split up.'

She stared at him and opened her mouth as if to protest but something about the expression in his eyes silenced her.

'Oh, I know things had been rocky between us for some time,' he said quickly, 'and I know I was pretty insufferable most of the time, but I really did love you, Ali, and I couldn't believe it when you left me.'

In the silence that followed the only sounds were Boy Blue's purring and the ticking of the clock.

'For some considerable time,' Connor went on at last, 'I was even arrogant enough to think you would be back. My male pride was badly hurt, you see—' he pulled a face '—and I didn't want to admit to anyone that I actually missed you.'

'And did you?' she asked quietly. 'Miss me, I mean?'

'If only you knew.' He lowered his head for a moment and continued stroking Boy Blue and then, looking up again, he said, 'I went through a bad patch, Ali. Once I'd got over the initial shock of you going

and come to terms with the fact that you had left me,
I started analysing why you'd gone and I slowly realised
how irresponsible and immature I'd been.'

Watching him closely, Ali saw the pain and shame
in his eyes. 'I didn't think things would ever get any
better,' she said quietly.

'They probably wouldn't have done if you hadn't
shocked me into seeing just how bad things were,' he
said grimly. 'Anyway,' he continued when she
remained silent, 'I became pretty desperate, so desperate
in fact that eventually I contacted your mother.'

'My mother. . .?' Ali's head jerked up in startled
surprise.

'Yes,' Connor nodded. 'I swallowed my pride and
phoned her.'

'What did she say?' Suddenly she was curious.

'She more or less told me to leave you alone,' he
said wryly.

'She said that?' Ali stared at him in surprise. She
had known her mother had had reservations about her
living with Connor but she hadn't thought she would
go that far.

'Yes,' he went on, 'she said she felt by then that you
were just beginning to get your life sorted out, that you
had got over me and that the last thing you would want
would be for me to mess things up again. . .' He paused.
'Had you got over me Ali,' he asked, 'as soon as that?'

She swallowed. 'This is meant to be your explanation,' she said drily.

'OK.' He gave a rueful little smile. 'Well, I tried. I
really tried, Ali. I did my best to forget you and over
a period of time I went out with a few other girls. . .'

She looked up sharply but he carried on talking.

'. . .but none of those relationships really worked.
Slowly I began to realise that they didn't work because
I was still missing you. . . I was still in love with

you. What we had was very special, Ali. . .' He paused. 'Anyway, eventually I tried again to find out where you had gone.'

'Not my mother again. . .?' She felt her lips twitch.

'Oh, no, not your mother again.' He shook his head. 'I'm not that much of a masochist. No, this time I tried through the old hospital grapevine. I drew blank after blank.' He went on after a moment, 'It was as if you'd vanished off the face of the earth. Then one day, quite by chance, I met Rupert Jameson—remember Rupert?'

'Could I ever forget? He was nearly as wild as you.'

'Yes, well—' Connor pulled a face '—I came across Rupert again and he told me someone he knew had been involved in a slight accident on the motorway near Denehurst. They'd been brought into A and E at St Mark's and had recognised you.'

'You couldn't go into hiding in this country, could you,' said Ali drily, 'even if you wanted to?'

Connor grinned. 'I'm glad of that,' he said and, growing serious again, he went on, 'It was the first break I'd had, so I followed it up. I came down to Denehurst and found out for myself that you did indeed work here. . .'

'When was that?' she asked, her curiosity getting the better of her.

'Late last year. . .near Christmas, in fact,' he said.

'What?' She stared at him. 'As long ago as that?'

He nodded and looked, she thought, sheepish.

'So why didn't you say anything? Come to see me?' she demanded.

'And what would you have done if I had?' He raised his eyebrows

'Well. . .' she trailed off.

'I can tell you exactly,' he said. 'You would have either refused to see me or, if you had, you would have sent me packing in no uncertain terms.'

'I. . .'

'You would, Ali. You know you would.'

She shrugged and looked out of the window.

'I decided,' he went on, 'that drastic measures were called for. I knew I had to establish myself in a situation where you couldn't send me packing. First of all, I looked at the job situation at St Mark's but there was absolutely nothing going at all. I then looked a little further afield and found a position as a locum in Winchester.'

She turned her head and stared at him in amazement. 'You did that?'

He nodded. 'I was determined,' he said. 'The next thing I did was to start looking for a property in the area.'

'Were you at Greyfriars then?' she asked quickly.

He shook his head. 'No, I had a very humble little bedsit just outside Winchester at that point. Anyway, I scoured the estate agents, found Langstone Farm Cottage and put in an offer. My offer was accepted and I found Tom Simmonds, who was willing to undertake the necessary renovations.'

'I can't believe you were prepared to go to those lengths just on the off chance that I might. . .' She shook her head in disbelief.

'I felt when the time came for me to lay my cards on the table,' Connor went on quietly, 'I needed to be able to prove to you that I had mended my ways. I decided there was no better way than to buy a property and put down some roots at last.'

'So how did you get to St Mark's?' Ali asked after a moment. She was beginning to wonder if she was in some sort of dream.

'I admit that was a lucky break,' admitted Connor. 'I had continued to scour the job advertisements and I knew by the law of averages that eventually something

would come up at St Mark's. I must admit I hadn't
thought I would get so lucky that it would be in A and
E itself. Anyway, when the CO post came up I applied,
went for an interview and got the job.'

'So that day when you came in to see Harvey. . .?'

'Was the day I knew I'd got the job,' he admitted.

'Why did you pretend to be surprised when you saw
me?' she demanded.

'I knew I still had to tread carefully. I wasn't sure
what sort of reception I would get from you. As it
happened, my caution was not without due cause.' He
smiled. 'You didn't exactly roll out the red carpet,
did you?'

She flushed. 'I was shocked. . .' she protested.

'At that point I decided my luck had run out,' said
Connor ruefully. 'Until then things had gone so
smoothly, too smoothly, I guess. I knew you might be
upset at seeing me. I hadn't quite bargained for just
how upset.'

'I had just started to get my life back together,
Connor,' she protested. 'And suddenly there you were.
I didn't want all that pain again.'

'So are you saying you had got over me?' he said
softly.

'Let's just say I was doing my best,' she retorted.
'The idea of working alongside you, being with you
and seeing you every day. . . Honestly, I really didn't
think I could cope with that again.'

'So you threatened to leave.'

She nodded.

'I must admit I hadn't bargained for that,' he said
thoughtfully. 'I didn't realise you would be prepared to
go to those lengths.'

'I was desperate. . .!'

'So was I!' He gave a short laugh. 'There I was. I'd
taken a tremendous gamble—new house and a new job

just to be near you. And there you were—talking of moving on again. I knew I had to do something quickly, very quickly, or I would be in danger of finding myself back at square one. That was when I gambled again—'

'And lied to me—'

'—and invented the idea of another woman,' he concluded firmly. 'Like I said though, Ali,' he continued, 'it worked—you are still here, still in Denehurst and still at St Mark's.'

She remained silent for a long time, once more staring out of the window and watching the sky as it changed from blue to a deep crimson. At last, with a sigh, she looked at him again and found that he was watching her. Boy Blue was fast asleep, curled into a ball on his lap.

'So, did Maggie know?' she asked.

He nodded.

'For how long?'

'A few weeks,' he admitted.

'How? Why? I don't understand.'

'I sensed Maggie was disgusted with me,' he said. 'I could tell she thought I was cruel by staying in Denehurst and planning to marry another woman right under your nose, so I confided in her. . .'

'And what was her reaction to that?' asked Ali sceptically.

'She thought I stood a good chance of getting you back but she warned me to tread carefully—that you had been very hurt and were still vulnerable.'

'What was all that about the barbeque?' she said suspiciously.

'Maggie helped me to try to create an atmosphere. . .' he said at last, 'the same atmosphere as the night we met. . .'

'Even down to the saxophone solo?' She raised one eyebrow.

He grinned sheepishly, then nodded. 'Yes, pity it didn't work. . .'

'Actually, Connor,' she said quietly, 'that is where you are wrong.'

He looked up sharply, so sharply that Boy Blue stirred and stretched, annoyed at having been disturbed. 'What do you mean?' he said.

'That night of the barbeque,' she said, 'was the closest it came to the old magic. I wanted you again that night, Connor,' she admitted at last.

He was silent for a moment, then he lifted his head and looked at her. 'I know you did,' he said, and there was no boastful triumph in the simple statement, 'as much as I wanted you.'

'Then why didn't. . .?' she frowned.

'Why didn't I take advantage of the situation?'

She nodded helplessly.

He sighed. 'I longed to. But I knew if I did, that would be the end. It might have been all right at the time but in the cold light of day you would have hated me. I knew I mustn't rush you, Ali. I knew I had to take things much more slowly than that or you would think I was still as impetuous and immature as I was three years ago. But, of course, what I wasn't prepared for was the unforeseen.'

'Unforeseen?'

'Yes, Maggie going into hospital, that meeting with Ted and his assumption that all was well between us. . .' He paused, then slowly, deliberately, he said, 'Now that it's all out in the open, Ali, and there is no more pretence, could all be well between us again?'

She continued to stare at him, her brain in turmoil.

Easing Boy Blue from his lap, he stood up.

'Don't answer that now,' he said.

'But. . .'

'I want you to think about it,' he said. 'Think about

it carefully. I want you to be absolutely certain that it's what you want.'

Ali stood up and faced him. 'That what is what I want?' she said.

'To marry me,' he said, 'and to help me make Langstone Farm Cottage into a home for our family.' Moving closer, he cupped her face in his hands and looked down into her eyes. 'I'm going now,' he said, 'going—to give you time to think—because, if I stay, within five minutes neither of us will be in any fit state to think.'

She remained very still as he left the room, still not moving even when she heard the click of the front door, but at the sound of his car as he started the engine she sank down onto her chair again.

When Boy Blue found that Connor had indeed abandoned him he transferred his affections to Ali and settled himself comfortably on her lap while she sat in the gathering twilight, trying to make sense of all that had happened.

If she was honest she was still reeling from the sheer ingenuity of Connor's plan of campaign, of the lengths he had gone to to try to get her back. And, she thought with a little stab of pleasure, there now was no other woman to worry about, and there never had been.

Connor had told her that he loved her, always had, and wanted to marry her—wanted her to live at Langstone Farm Cottage with him and to start a family. They'd never even mentioned children before—she hadn't dared. Connor would have seen it as yet another attempt to tie him down. Could he really have changed that much?

She shifted restlessly in her chair. He really did appear to be a reformed character these days, to have curtailed the wilder aspects of his nature—but could she trust him again? Should she trust him? He had, after all, lied to her—invented the existence of another woman to make her stay at St Mark's.

And what of her? How did she feel? When he had first appeared in her life again she had been horrified. Why? Had it been simply because she hadn't wanted to work with him? Had it been because she no longer loved him? Had grown to hate him? She knew that it was none of these things; knew that deep down it was precisely the opposite. She hadn't wanted to work with him, to have him around again, because she had never got over him, because deep inside she still loved him and instinctively she had known she couldn't bear to have him around if that love was to go unfulfilled.

And now he had told her that he wanted her, loved her, so why should she even hesitate? Why was she afraid to love him again?

With a sigh, she finally lifted Boy Blue who, disgusted at being disturbed yet again, leapt to the floor and stalked off into the kitchen. Then she stood up, walked into the hall and locked the front door before slowly making her way up the stairs to bed.

The next day A and E was so busy that Ali hardly had time to pass the time of day with Connor, let alone discuss the future.

Poor air quality had brought in a spate of patients suffering from asthma attacks and an early morning mist had been responsible for two road traffic accidents, involving one fatality and numerous injuries.

'Is Maggie having her op this morning?' asked Jessica as she helped Ali to set up a nebuliser.

'Yes.' Ali nodded. In spite of her own concerns her friend hadn't been far from her thoughts for one minute that morning.

'I've bought her an African violet,' said Jessica.

'Harvey said I could probably pop up later and give it to her.'

'That's kind.' Ali smiled at the student. 'I shall go up when the shift's over. . . You look happy this morning,' she added noting the girl's flushed cheeks and shining eyes. . .

'I went out with Joe last night,' Jessica replied simply.

'No need to ask if you had a good time.'

'I thought it was the end of the world when Dave and I split up,' said Jessica, 'but now. . .well, Joe is so different!'

At that moment Connor looked into the cubicle where they were working. 'Everything all right in here?' he said.

'Yes, fine, thanks.' Ali met his gaze and was forced to look away.

'Right,' he said, 'I'll leave you to it, then.'

As he moved out of the cubicle and drew the curtains behind him, Ali looked at Jessica and saw that the girl had obviously seen the look that had just passed between her and Connor.

'I think,' said Jessica with a sigh, 'that Dr Steven's is absolutely gorgeous. Pity he's committed elsewhere. If he wasn't, I could go for him myself—if I didn't have Joe, of course,' she added hurriedly when she saw Ali's raised eyebrows. 'So, who is it?' she said after a moment.

'Who is what?' asked Ali.

'This woman he's committed to?'

'Er, actually there is no woman,' said Ali.

'Really?' Jessica's eyes widened in sudden interest. 'So does that mean that you and he. . .?'

'I really don't know,' said Ali, trying to sound brisk but only too aware that her cheeks were suddenly burning.

'It does. . .doesn't it?' said Jessica excitedly. 'He's asked you, hasn't he?'

'Asked me what?' said Ali, trying to remain cool as even the patient began to show interest, in spite of the distress from her asthma attack.

'I don't know. Asked you out. Asked you to live with him again. Marry him. . .or whatever.' The girl's eyes were like saucers now and she could hardly contain her excitement.

'Shh, Jessica,' said Ali in embarrassment, 'please keep your voice down. I don't want everyone knowing.'

'So it's true, then! He has asked you!'

'Yes, it's true,' muttered Ali, 'but please keep it to yourself, Jessica.'

'Oh, yes, yes, of course I will.' Jessica clasped her hands together and smiled rapturously at the patient, who lifted the nebuliser mask for a moment and smiled back.

Ali wasn't sure how she got through the rest of the shift but as the day wore on she became increasingly convinced that, in spite of her asking Jessica not to say anything, the girl had told the rest of the staff. It was just little things—a speculative glance from Beth, a knowing smile from Harvey, a cryptic remark from Joe—things that at any other time she would have ignored but today, with what was happening, took on a whole new meaning.

In the end she was glad when the shift was over, glad that Connor was preoccupied with the relative of a patient in the interview room and glad that she could escape alone to see Maggie.

She found her friend with her eyes closed, her auburn hair spread out on the mountain of pillows. Beside her on the locker stood the African violet and a vase of yellow rosebuds.

As Ali looked down at her, Maggie opened her eyes.

'Hi,' she said.

'Hi, yourself,' said Ali, bending over and kissing Maggie's cheek. 'How are you feeling?'

'A bit sore—but I'm still all there if you know what I mean.'

Ali smiled and nodded.

'Tim Bartholomew's just been down to see me. . .'

'And. . .?'

'He said he's as sure as he can be that it was harmless. I'll have to wait for histology, of course, but. . .' She shrugged, then winced.

'Brought you some sweet peas from the stall,' said Ali, then added with a laugh, 'Looks like you'll be able to start your own stall soon.'

'Yes.' Maggie turned her head and looked at her locker. 'Jessica brought the violet and the rosebuds are from Ted. He always sent me yellow roses. . .'

Ali stayed for about fifteen minutes but as Maggie's eyelids drooped again she stood up. 'I'm going now,' she said, 'so that you can get some rest. I'm sure Ted will be in later to see you.'

Maggie smiled and nodded. 'Bye, Ali,' she said sleepily, 'and thanks for coming.' Then, as Ali moved away from the bed, she said, 'Oh, Ali. . .'

'Yes?' Ali stopped and turned.

'I'm so pleased,' said Maggie, 'about you and Connor. Jessica told me. So pleased. . . Be happy. . . Don't waste any more years. . . Life's too short, you know. . .' Her eyelids finally closed.

Ali stood watching her for a while. Maggie might be asleep, might not know she was there, but when at last she moved away she felt that she had the answer she had been struggling to find.

Connor was waiting for her in Reception. He knew where she had been and he raised his eyebrows as she stepped out of the lift.

She stared at him for a long moment, then nodded and smiled and in that moment they both knew that the question of Maggie's health was not the only question that had been answered.

He held out his hand and, as he took hers, he said, 'Come on, I'll take you home. . .'

They talked for hours that evening in the little house in Church Close. They shared a meal and a bottle of wine and still they talked, filling in all the gaps of the last three years. They talked of the past, exorcised a few ghosts, exploded a few myths and ironed out certain difficulties and uncertainties.

'I really have reformed, you know,' said Connor at last, leaning back in his chair, 'if you will only give me the chance to prove it.'

'Actually,' replied Ali, 'that is something that has been bothering me.'

'What?' Connor looked startled.

'That you might have reformed too much.'

He stared at her for a moment then, as he saw her lips twitch and he grasped the meaning of her words, he pushed his chair back and stood up. 'Ah, now, if it's that you're worrying about,' he said, 'I can see it's that I need to be proving.' He moved round the table and, taking her hands, raised her to her feet, stared down into her eyes and then, with a groan, almost roughly pulled her into his arms and covered her mouth with his.

With a sigh, Ali parted her lips and closed her eyes, daring for the first moment since he'd walked into St Mark's to relax and to lower her guard. Allowing her fingers to sink into the dark tangle of his hair and her body to melt into his, she was only too aware of the hardening response of his own body.

'I want you so much,' he groaned between kisses.

'You can't believe how much I've wanted you. . .ached for you. . .'

'Yes, Connor, I can,' she whispered as his hands moved urgently over her body, moulding her hips, drawing her even closer, 'because I've wanted you too. . . so much. . .so many times. . .' Her own desire flared to match his and she was vaguely aware that he was struggling with the buttons on her blouse. Without any hesitation she helped him and somehow, only moments later—with a frenzied trail of clothing on the stairs behind them—they found themselves in the bedroom.

As the last garments slid to the floor, Connor lifted her into his arms and carried her to the bed.

'My darling girl,' he said as he lowered her onto the soft duvet and stretched out beside her, 'I thought this moment would never come. I really thought at times I had lost you forever.'

'Connor. . .' she whispered and, turning to him, gave herself up to sheer joy as he aroused and caressed her, leading her down the path they had trodden so many times before—the path that led to ecstasy.

When at last they became one it was like a homecoming of the senses, the sweetness so piercing that she wondered how she could ever have doubted him—how she could have survived so long without him.

The intensity of their loving steadily gained momentum as they explored the very depths of each other's souls, until finally, when their passion exploded in a rush of emotion, Connor called out her name.

When it was all over the peace between them was so perfect that she knew in her heart that this was how it would always be.

Much later, as he nibbled her earlobe, he said, lazily 'So, have I reformed too much for you?'

'No, you are still as wild as ever,' she sighed. 'Not that I'd want you any other way,' she added hastily.

'Thank goodness for that!' He gave an exaggerated sigh. 'I had an awful feeling that these reforms of yours might include what goes on under the bedclothes.' As he spoke he pulled the duvet over their heads.

Ali shrieked as he made it perfectly apparent what he intended next, and then suddenly she froze.

'What is it?' he said, lifting his head.

'Boy Blue,' whispered Ali.

'What. . .?'

'He's on the bed. . .' She pushed back the duvet a little as Boy Blue crept stealthily up the bed, peered at the two of them and then, apparently satisfied, retreated to the foot of the bed where, purring happily, he curled himself into a ball and settled down to sleep.

'He obviously approves,' said Ali with a laugh.

'Ah, well, that's all right, then,' said Connor. Pulling up the duvet again, he added, 'Now tell me, where were we?'

'As if you needed reminding. . .' she replied with a sigh.

MILLS & BOON®

Medical Romance™

COMING NEXT MONTH

IF YOU NEED ME... by Caroline Anderson
Audley Memorial Hospital

Joe, now an Obs & Gynae consultant, had been fostered by Thea's parents so when, years later, she turned up on his doorstep, homeless and eight months pregnant, naturally he took her in. But behaving like a brother was difficult....

A SURGEON TO TRUST by Janet Ferguson

Anna's ex-husband had been a womaniser, and much as she liked working with surgeon Simon, she found it very hard to trust him, particularly when appearances suggested he might be just the same kind of man.

VALENTINE'S HUSBAND by Josie Metcalfe

Valentine dreaded her birthday, for it was her wedding anniversary too, a stark reminder of her husband and child, lost in a car accident. Escorting an old lady to France was the perfect escape, until she met Guy, a Casualty doctor, and Madame's grandson!

WINGS OF PASSION by Meredith Webber
Flying Doctors

After losing Nick, socialite Allysha had turned her life around and become a pilot for the RFDS, confident of her skills, but with no social life—until, quite unexpectedly, Nick arrived to replace Matt. How was she to convince him the change was real and lasting?

FREE!

FOUR FREE
specially selected
Medical Romance™ novels
PLUS a Mystery Gift
when you return this card...

Return this coupon and we'll send you 4 Medical Romance novels and a mystery gift absolutely FREE! We'll even pay the postage and packing for you.

We're making you this offer to introduce you to the benefits of the Reader Service™ – FREE home delivery of brand-new Medical Romance novels, at least a month before they are available in the shops, FREE gifts and a monthly Newsletter packed with information.

Accepting these FREE books and gift places you under no obligation to buy, you may cancel at any time, even after receiving just your free shipment. Simply complete the coupon below and send it to:

MILLS & BOON READER SERVICE, FREEPOST, CROYDON, SURREY, CR9 3WZ.

No stamp needed

Yes, please send me 4 free Medical Romance novels and a mystery gift. I understand that unless you hear from me, I will receive 4 superb new titles every month for just £2.10* each, postage and packing free. I am under no obligation to purchase any books and I may cancel or suspend my subscription at any time, but the free books and gift will be mine to keep in any case. (I am over 18 years of age)

M7XE

Ms/Mrs/Miss/Mr _____

Address _____

_____

_____ Postcode _____

Offer closes 31st July 1997. We reserve the right to refuse an application. *Prices and terms subject to change without notice. Offer only valid in UK and Ireland and is not available to current subscribers to this series. **Readers in Ireland please write to: P.O. Box 4546, Dublin 24.** Overseas readers please write for details.

You may be mailed with offers from other reputable companies as a result of this application. Please tick box if you would prefer not to receive such offers. ☐

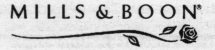